HEROINES OF JIANGYONG

HEROINES *of* JIANGYONG

CHINESE NARRATIVE BALLADS IN WOMEN'S SCRIPT

Translation & Introduction by

WILT L. IDEMA

UNIVERSITY OF WASHINGTON PRESS   SEATTLE & LONDON

The publication of *Heroines of Jiangyong: Chinese Narrative Ballads in Women's Script* was generously supported by a grant from the Chiang Ching-Kuo Foundation for International Scholarly Exchange, and by the Donald R. Ellegood International Publications Endowment.

© 2009 by the University of Washington Press
Printed in the United States of America
Designed by Ashley Saleeba
14 13 12 11 10 09   5 4 3 2 1

UNIVERSITY OF WASHINGTON PRESS
PO Box 50096, Seattle, WA 98145
www.washington.edu/uwpress

The paper used in this publication is acid-free and 90 percent recycled from at least 50 percent post-consumer waste. It meets the minimum requirements of American National Standard for Information Sciences—Permanence of Paper for Printed Library Materials, ANSI Z39.48–1984.

LIBRARY OF CONGRESS CATALOGING-IN-PUBLICATION DATA
Heroines of Jiangyong: Chinese narrative ballads in women's script /
translation and Introduction by Wilt L. Idema.
p. cm.
Includes bibliographical references.
ISBN 978-0-295-98841-2 (hbk. : alk. paper) — ISBN 978-0-295-98842-9 (pbk. : alk. paper)
1. Chinese poetry—Women authors—Translations into English.   2. Chinese poetry—China—Jiangyong Xian.   3. Chinese poetry—20th century.   I. Idema, W. L. (Wilt L.)
II. Title: Chinese narrative ballads in women's script.
PL2658.E3H45 2009
895.1'1520809287—dc22   2008037004

COVER: "Two elderly practitioners of women's script, Gao Yixian and Yi Nianhua, exchange their innermost feelings." *Guizhong qiji—Zhongguo nüshu* (2005), 35.
TITLE PAGE: A handkerchief with a third day letter in women's script, originally in the possession of He Yanxin and currently preserved at the Museum of Ethnology, Academia Sinica. (Photo: Liu Fei-wen)

CONTENTS

ACKNOWLEDGMENTS

THIS BOOK COULD NOT HAVE COME ABOUT WITHOUT THE painstaking work many Chinese scholars have done in collecting and transcribing the manuscripts in women's script. Through their efforts, they have made the writings of the women of Jiangyong available to a much wider readership, in China and abroad.

The invitation of Vibeke Børdahl to attend the International Workshop on Oral Literature in Modern China (Copenhagen, August 29–31, 1996) was a major stimulus for me to look more closely at the narrative ballads in the women's script manuscripts. As a result, I not only presented a paper on this topic at the conference (a revised version of which serves as the introduction to this volume) but also prepared Dutch translations of some of these ballads, which are included in my *Vrouwenschrift: Vriendschap, huwelijk en wanhoop van Chinese vrouwen, opgetekend in een eigen schrift* [Women's script: Friendship, love, and frustration of Chinese women, recorded in a script of their own]. This experience strengthened my conviction that these ballads, both as moving narratives and as texts selected by women for women, well merited a full translation into English.

The readers for the University of Washington Press provided me with excellent feedback, and the extensive notes of Fei-wen Liu on the introduction and each of the translations were especially helpful. As before, working with the highly professional staff at the University of Washington Press was a pleasure. A special word of thanks is due to my copy editor, Laura Iwasaki, who has carefully vetted my English. I alone, however, take full responsibility for all remaining errors.

Last but not least, I would like to express my thanks to the friendly staffs of the Library of the Leiden Sinological Institute and the Harvard-Yenching Library, who have been extremely efficient in providing me with the materials I requested, even if these had to be fetched from the other side of the globe.

HEROINES OF JIANGYONG

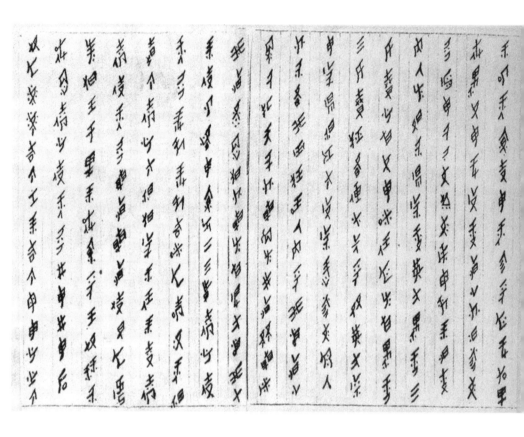

A passage in women's script from *The Karmic Affinity of Liang Shanbo and Zhu Yingtai* in the handwriting of Gao Yinxian, reproduced from Zhao Liming, ed., *Zhongguo nüshu heji* (Beijing: Zhonghua shuju, 2005), vol. 2, p. 1404.

INTRODUCTION

WOMEN'S SCRIPT

THE SMALL COUNTY OF JIANGYONG, IN SOUTHERNMOST Hunan, is unique in China in one remarkable aspect: up to the middle of the twentieth century, its women wrote down their poems and ballads, complaints and tales in a script of their own. As in the rest of China, the few literate men in Jiangyong studied and wrote in standard Chinese characters, and their way of writing was referred to in the county as "men's script" (*nanshu*). The women of Jiangyong, however, used a syllabic script in which each sign stood for a distinctive unit of sound in the local Chinese dialect. This script was known as "women's script" (*nüshu*). The writings in this script are equally unique. While scholars in recent years have increasingly become aware of the richness and variety of writings by women in traditional China, it must be admitted that the overwhelming majority of these poems and songs, plays and ballads were authored by elite women from the Jiangnan area, especially the great cities of Suzhou and Hangzhou.[1] Writings in women's script from the nineteenth and twentieth centuries, however, present us with peasant women speaking their own minds and in their own words, unmediated by modern intellectuals, whether native party cadres or foreign anthropologists.

Not surprisingly, women's script created quite a stir when it first became known outside Jiangyong in the late 1980s, and at that time, the media presented women's script as a secret language of women. Women's script, however, was not a language, just a system for writing the local dialect, and it was not secret either. Some writings in women's script, such as letters between sworn sisters, were not intended to be seen by men, while other writings, such as Third-Day Letters, long songs of felicitation sent to the bride by friends and relatives after her wedding, were a matter of pride and were publicly displayed. Many of the songs and ballads written down in women's script were sung at public festivities, and we also know of one or two men who learned to write women's script. But even though it was not secret as such, women's script was to all practical purposes used exclusively by women. In addition, outside the confines of the few villages in Jiangyong where women's script flourished, people were unable to recognize it as a script, let alone read it.

Some Chinese scholars believe that the women's script of Jiangyong derives from the official writing system in use during the days of the mythic Emperor Shun, whereas some of their more sober-minded colleagues have drawn attention to similarities between women's script signs and oracle bone inscriptions. Others have discussed the possibility of a relationship with the writing systems of various southwestern ethnic minorities. Local legends trace the origin of women's script back to a local girl who had been selected for the imperial harem and wanted to communicate her misery to her family in such a way that no outsiders would be able to read her letters, or to a girl who had been thrown in prison and wanted to contact her relatives, or to a girl who just wanted to contact her friends.[2] However, we most likely have to follow scholars such as Gong Zhebing and Zhao Liming, who conclude that the Jiangyong women's script originated from Chinese characters and, by continuous simplification, developed into a syllabic script for the local dialect. Women's script counts more than a thousand signs, one for every syllable of the local dialect; it writes sound, not meaning. The script may well have been a very local and relatively short-lived phenomenon: there is no indication whatsoever that it was used outside one part of Jiangyong and some bordering communities; it probably had come into being only by the early years of the nineteenth century, and essentially became a thing of the past following the establishment of the People's Republic of China in 1949 and the attendant demise of traditional local culture.[3] Once the tradition had practically disappeared, major efforts were undertaken to revive the tradition to some degree. Such attempts, one suspects, while partly motivated by local pride, are also instigated by commercial considerations, as the fame of women's script has given local tourism a major boost.[4]

In traditional Jiangyong, women rarely participated in work outdoors; instead, they spent their time on household chores and on spinning, weaving, and embroidery. These latter activities often were group activities, during which one of the women might relieve the boredom of the repetitive task by chanting songs and ballads in women's script. Also, during the days preceding a wedding, women would congregate in the house of the bride-to-be and spend their time chanting songs and ballads. The first known explicit reference to women's script (from 1931) links it to a local temple festival during which women recited their songs. Until 1949, some temples also doubled as a lending library of sorts: women placed their own writings there and took home other women's writings for reading and copying before returning them. If one of the younger girls showed an interest in learning the script, she usually would be coached by a member of the older generation, her mother or an aunt. Some of the women who had mastered the script would also compose new texts. All texts are rhymed ballads, and by far the most common line is the seven-syllable line of traditional balladry that is found all over China. As in all oral and semi-oral traditions, the language tends to be highly formulaic.[5] Some women combined a mastery of women's script with a rudimentary knowledge of regular Chinese characters (allowing them to transcribe such materials into women's script), but for girls, opportunities for regular schooling were almost nonexistent before 1949, and the ability to read and write women's script was highly prized in local society.[6]

Altogether, some five hundred texts in women's script have been preserved, ranging from four-line poems to long autobiographical songs and narrative ballads of hundreds of lines. One of the most complete collections of materials in women's script, Zhao Liming's *Great Collection of China's Women's Script Texts* (Zhongguo nüshu jicheng) of 1992, divides its materials thematically into ten sections. One large section (twenty-two texts) consists of letters exchanged between sworn sisters. A very large section (fifty-six texts), titled "Marriage Songs," consists of the many short songs a bride chants while taking leave of her parental home. Another, even larger section (eighty-two texts) consists of Third-Day Letters. The section "Folksongs" has eighty-seven items, while "Riddles" contains forty-seven short songs. Thirty-two further items have been classified as "Narrative Songs," and the collection also contains thirty modern letters and thirty-six autobiographical ballads, both long and short. "Religious Songs" is by far the smallest section with only seven items.[7] At the very end, twenty-nine works have been grouped together as adaptations of works originally composed in Chinese characters. This section consists of a few widely known classical poems, some versified moral tracts for women, and a number of narrative ballads.[8] Some of these ballads had been transliterated, not once, but twice, suggesting their popularity among Jiangyong women.

The overwhelming majority of the currently known manuscripts in women's script, it should be pointed out, are of a very recent date. Many date only from the 1980s, when scholars asked the few women who still knew how to read and write women's script to record texts from memory. The two most important informants have been Gao Yinxian (1902–1990) and Yi Nianhua (1907–1991). Yet another important informant, Yang Huanyi, died as late as 2004.[9] Many manuscripts were willfully destroyed during the years of the Cultural Revolution (1966–76), while other manuscripts disappeared upon the deaths of their owners, who had them burned or placed in their coffins so they could enjoy their favorite texts in the afterlife. Some of the narrative ballads, however, had already been transcribed by Hu Cizhu, who died in 1976, well before the upsurge of interest in women's script in the 1980s, and some other texts were available to researchers in 1982,[10] which perhaps suggests that the selection in this respect reflects the preferences of the local women rather than pressure from local cultural workers. (Attempts in the 1950s to have women sing the praises of socialism in women's script were not particularly successful.)

Since their discovery by the outside world, writings in women's script have attracted considerable scholarship, in both Chinese and other languages. Chinese scholars have collected manuscripts and urged the few remaining women who could write the script to record from memory the texts that had been lost. These texts have been published in large volumes, often with a transliteration in Chinese characters and in the International Phonetic Alphabet. Chinese scholars also have speculated extensively on the earliest origins of women's script and the possibility of cultural influences from non-Han ethnic groups. Both Chinese and Western scholars have been intrigued by the local culture of sworn sisterhood and the local marriage system.[11] Anthropological research has tried to place the various types of women's script writings in the context of local society and custom, relying heavily on the information provided by the elderly women who had grown up when women's script and its literature were a thriving tradition.[12] Others have looked at the rich body of autobiographical ballads, which as a rule are mostly given over to cataloging the sufferings a woman endured as daughter, daughter-in-law, and widowed mother. The lives of the women of Jiangyong even inspired a best-selling novel in English.[13]

This volume focuses on a segment of writings in women's script that so far has been largely neglected in the English-language secondary scholarship, namely, the versified moral tracts and narrative ballads that were so popular with Jiangyong women that they transliterated the texts into women's script. The originals of the adaptations in this volume were printed in cheap little booklets commonly called "songbooks" (*changben*). The ballads uniformly employ a seven-syllable line; their language is highly formulaic, and their subject matter is traditional.[14] The simple form and formulaic language, however, apparently appealed to the women of Jiangyong. All the transcribed ballads concern well-known stories that are centuries if not millennia old and are also known from other parts of China. While these texts therefore are not original, the selection made by Jiangyong women may tell us much about which popular stories especially appealed to them. The corpus of ballads transcribed into women's script is the only example known to me of ballads selected by women for women, and as these ballads clearly reflect the concerns of a specifically female and rural audience, this body of texts well merits our attention.[15]

TRACTS AND BALLADS

Before going any further, I should stress that I, unlike some other scholars of women's script, have never visited Jiangyong, the home of women's script, let alone done any research there. I do not speak the local dialect and do not read women's script as such. For my translations, I relied exclusively on published transcriptions in Chinese characters of writings originally composed in women's script. I had at my disposal four large-scale publications that reproduce the women's script writings together with transcriptions in Chinese characters (two of the publications also provided transcriptions in the International Phonetic Alphabet); together, they include practically all known manuscripts in women's script. The first three publications are Gong Zhebing's *Women's Script* (Nüshu) of 1991; Xie Zhimin's *The Mystery of Jiangyong's Women's Script* (Jiangyong nüshu zhi mi) of 1991; and Zhao Liming's *Great Collection of China's Women's Script Texts* of 1992. In 2005, Zhao Liming published *A Complete Collection of China's Women's Script Texts* (Zhongguo nüshu heji) in five volumes; it contains photographic reproductions of all known women's script manuscripts, arranged by writer, together with a transliteration in Chinese characters of each text.

The translations in this volume are based primarily on Zhao Liming's 1992 work. However, the appendices in Xie Zhimin's *The Mystery of Jiangyong's Women's Script* contain much more extensive materials on the local society and dialect than the other works do.

The stories the women of Jiangyong selected for transcription into women's script present a narrow range of positive and negative role models for women. Their examples of womanly virtues and vices make it clear that a woman's lot is hard work and silent suffering, physical discomfort, and the ubiquitous danger of rape. No virtue is stressed more strongly than chaste loyalty to one's husband, especially an absent husband. In almost all the stories, the woman is the strong character, and "the courage, wisdom, and initiative of the heroines form an interesting contrast with the relative timidity and incompetence of the male characters."[16]

Some texts deal explicitly with the unfairness of socially sanctioned gender relations but conclude that gender roles are given and cannot be transgressed in this life. Any female who attempts to join male society has to fail, especially if she allows herself to be influenced by passion. However, a woman who is willing to forgo sexuality may hope to be reborn as a man. As these texts do not reflect an active desire to change existing gender relations, it may not be appropriate to label them "feminist," as has been done on occasion.[17] However, the selection of texts and their adaptation clearly reflect a female view of traditional society and "show a keen perception of the subtle secrets of the inner spiritual world of women."[18] Anne McLaren concludes that "it might be best to consider *nüshu*, and the performances that lie behind it, as a gender-specific genre for the ritualized expression of a feminine code of endurance in adversity. By lamenting her hardship in a culturally approved way, a woman gained status for her talent in *nüshu* and also a network of sworn sisters, who provided moral support and sympathy beyond the natal and marital family." "In this woman's line of oral transmission, one can indeed hear 'women's voices,' not so much as individuals but as a collectivity."[19] Most recently, Liu Feiwen has argued that some texts, while clearly supporting traditional patriarchy, may yet acquire a subtle subversive potential in performance, such as when Third-Day Letters are collectively performed by married women, thereby strengthening their solidarity.[20]

What we do not find among the transcribed texts are stories of border warfare and of amorous conquest. In view of the popularity of these topics in popular drama, vernacular fiction, and ballad literature in general, this may at first seem surprising. However, on second thought, one realizes that these tales mostly serve to define male gender norms. In such stories, Chinese manhood endlessly defines and redefines, constructs and reconstructs itself by fighting off foreign foes, defeating time and again the various barbarians that encroach on Chinese soil, and by subjugating the enemy within by marrying and satisfying any number of women. Although many stories of amorous conquest were performed by female entertainers, that should not blind us to the predominantly male view of the universe expressed in such stories—their audience in the public domain of a teahouse was primarily male.

THE BURDENS OF THE FEMALE CONDITION

A number of didactic tracts spell out the moral duties of women. Chapter 1, "Admonitions for My Daughter" (Xunnü ci), admonishes a young girl against playfulness and urges her to be diligent at all times.[21] This ballad is a reworking of a poem by a local gentry woman, Pu Bixian (1804–1860).[22] The hardships of a married woman's life are spelled out in chapter 2, "The Ten Months of Pregnancy" (Shiyue huaitai),[23] which starts out by describing the physical discomforts that accompany each successive stage of pregnancy, continues with a gruesome sketch of the dangers of childbirth, and concludes with a survey of the parents' worries, especially the mother's, during the youth and adolescence of the child until he is married.[24] Chapter 3, "The Family Heirloom" (Chuanjiabao), covers the same ground but then continues with a description of grown-up sons who refuse to obey their parents' commands and insist on a division of the family property, after which they neglect their aging and ailing parents and, upon the parents' deaths, bury them without any sign of true grief.[25]

Both chapters 2 and 3 continue a vernacular tradition of more than a thousand years, going back at least to manuscripts of the ninth and tenth centuries discovered in a cave in Dunhuang. For instance, *Sutra-Explanation Text on the Sutra on the Importance of Parental Love* (Fumu enzhong jing jiangjingwen) describes at length, in prose and verse, the pains parents take on behalf of their children, in order to convince children that the obligations imposed by filial piety are but small repayment for the care their parents expended in raising them. In these two ballads, the description of parents' pains and worries, especially those of the mother, are intended to engender feelings of filial piety on the part of the children. However, as it is stressed that only those who act in a filial way can expect filial offspring, these texts also serve to impress on daughters-in-law the need to serve their parents-in-law with all required filiality.

The counter-image of the filial daughter-in-law is presented in chapter 4, "The Lazy Wife" (Lan poniang). This text describes at length the shortcomings of the lazy housewife. She has been spoiled by her parents. When her husband asks her to do something, she feigns illness, but as soon as he has left the house to work in the fields, she jumps out of her bed to raid the food chest. She cannot cook well or sew properly. When friends or relatives invite her to a party, she makes a laughingstock of herself because she does not have one decent set of clothes; however, she gobbles down all the good food. She cannot participate in conversation and when people ask her how much spinning she has done, she runs home and throws herself down on her bed. The author holds this lazy housewife up to scorn and ridicule.[26] Here, too, we are dealing with a tradition in vernacular literature that stretches back for more than a thousand years.[27]

STAND BY YOUR MAN

The texts mentioned above do not present much of a narrative. For a narrative illustration of an exemplary housewife, we turn to chapter 5, "The Tale of Third Sister" (Sangu ji). This is an adaptation of a ballad that purports to narrate a story that took place locally and recently, during the Guangxu reign (1875–1908). The earliest-known printing of this ballad probably dates to 1914;[28] however, the characters and incidents are so archetypal that the story might have taken place anywhere, anytime.

Third Sister is the daughter of a rich local family surnamed Wang. While her two elder sisters are both married to wealthy husbands, the family of Third Sister's husband (surnamed Xiao) has fallen upon hard times. Third Sister's mother therefore wants her to obtain a divorce, so she may then marry the rich and handsome young man across the street. When Third Sister indignantly rejects this proposal, her mother tells her to leave her house. Some years later, Third Sister's mother celebrates her fifty-first birthday, and the two elder sisters bring costly presents. Third Sister, who in the meantime has become the mother of a boy, also goes to her parents' house to pay her respects, but as her present is only very modest indeed, her mother does not allow her to sit with the guests but sends her to the kitchen and tells her to tend the fire in the oven. When the sons of her two elder sisters get hungry and ask for food, their grandmother gives them a leg of chicken, but when Third Sister's son also gets hungry and asks for something to eat, his grandmother gives him only an old radish. Third Sister complains about this unequal treatment, and her mother gives her a beating and tells her never to show up again.

Third Sister and her husband continue to exert themselves, and, as the gods help those who help themselves, they prosper and have another son. They buy houses and fields and encourage their sons to study. Eventually, both boys do well in the provincial examinations. In the meantime, disaster strikes the families of Third Sister's mother and sisters. The mother is even reduced to begging. One day, she finds herself in front of the gate of Third Sister's mansion. She implores her daughter for help, but Third Sister refuses her request and admits the wicked woman into the house only after her two sons have interceded on behalf of their grandmother. The remorseful old crone has the good grace to die within a year. She is given a fine grave, and her grandsons proceed to succeed in yet higher levels of examinations.[29]

This tale stresses a number of virtues. First of all, a wife should remain loyal to her husband, whatever misfortunes may befall them. Poverty is no reason for divorce, as any setback may be temporary. The wife of Zhu Maichen is the negative example par excellence of the wife who, in her short-sighted greed, insists on divorcing her husband during a spell of poverty; when he attains rank and riches, she commits suicide out of shame. This story had already been told in *History of the Han Dynasty* (Han shu), but we also encounter it as a fragmentary text among the women's script adaptations of songbook texts.[30]

Second, "The Tale of Third Sister" places great emphasis on the virtue of diligence and physical labor. Third Sister spends her time spinning, while her husband is described as hoeing the fields with an extra-heavy hoe. He grows a wide variety of crops, including wheat, barley, radishes, peanuts, and sweet potatoes. The gods take pity on the couple and direct them in their dreams to a hoard of gold and silver that lies buried in their fields. As soon as they have found this treasure, the devout couple thank the gods with the appropriate offerings.

Last but not least, the text stresses the virtue of filial piety. Third Sister may enjoy putting her mother in her place and reminding the old woman of her past boasts, but the daughter knows very well that eventually she will have to take her begging mother in and take care of her. The intervention of Third Sister's sons is needed only to help her save face—and to increase her sons' reputation for filial piety. Third Sister is not expected to love her mother; it is enough that she provides for the older woman's physical needs as long as she lives and builds a grave for her as soon as she has died. As filial parents have filial offspring, her sons reward her by achieving official positions.

FIDELITY TO ABSENT HUSBANDS

A significant number of transcribed ballads deal with the topic of fidelity to an absent husband. Many of these stories are represented by two manuscripts, further underlining the popularity of this theme.

The story "The Daughter of the Xiao Family" (Xiaoshi nü) is a version of the widespread tale of Liu Wenlong (or Liu Wenliang) and his loyal wife, known in dramatic form from as early as the fifteenth century.[31] In these dramatic versions, which are set during the reign of Emperor Yuan (r. 48–33 B.C.E.) of the Western Han dynasty (206 B.C.E.–8 C.E.), Liu Wenlong passes the metropolitan examinations as a "top of the list" (zhuangyuan). But when he then refuses to marry the prime minister's daughter because he is already married to lady Xiao, he is ordered to accompany Wang Zhaojun, who has just at that moment been given as a bride to the ruler of the Southern Xiongnu. Liu Wenlong later has a brilliant career in the land of the barbarians and marries a local princess, who eventually helps him return to China after she notices his enduring love for his first wife. Liu arrives back home just in time to prevent the forced remarriage of his wife. The plays stress equally the loyalty of husband and of wife and devote quite some space to the husband's heroic and amorous adventures in foreign lands.

In "The Daughter of the Xiao Family," the women's script version of the tale, Liu Wenliang is the only son of a rich family. When he grows up, he wants to leave his parents and pursue an official career. His parents try to keep him at home by providing him with a wife, lady Xiao, but four days after the wedding ceremony, he leaves anyway. As he departs, his bride urges him to return quickly and hands him three items by which they may recognize each other later. Liu Wenliang succeeds in the capital examinations and has a successful career that takes him to higher and higher posts, but for eighteen years, his parents and wife receive no news from him. His parents therefore assume that he has died and want their daughter-in-law to marry again so that they will have an adopted son-in-law who will look after them in their old age. Lady Xiao vows that she will remarry only if fishes climb up bamboos, the Yellow River runs dry, and horses grow horns. Her weeping attracts the attention of the god of the Taibai star, or Great White (the planet Venus), who descends to earth in the guise of an old man, listens to her story, and then sends a dream to Liu Wenliang. When Liu Wenliang has his dream interpreted, he realizes he must go home and requests leave to do so. Liu Wenliang arrives in his hometown and meets with his wife, who does not recognize him. She is about to commit suicide by drowning herself in the city moat, as her parents-in-law still insist on her remarrying. He proceeds to his home, where he identifies himself to his parents and his wife. All ends well as the couple has two sons, who both achieve high positions.[32] In this version of the tale, the story is told from the perspective of lady Xiao, and Liu Wenliang's prolonged absence is not due to his devotion to his wife but to his obsession with his career.

In this way, the story of lady Xiao and her absent husband shows many points of correspondence with the much older story of Qiu Hu and his wife, which was included by Liu Xiang (79–8 B.C.E.) in his *Biographies of Exemplary Women* (Lienü zhuan).[33] In later centuries, this tale was repeatedly adapted in all kinds of performative literature. It is represented among the transcribed texts in women's script by no fewer than three manuscripts, all titled "Lady Luo" (Luoshi nü), after Qiu Hu's wife. In these versions, Qiu Hu has been renamed Lu Qiuhu, and his wife's surname is derived from a Han-period ballad, in which a beautiful young woman called Qin Luofu, who is out in the fields picking mulberry leaves, rejects the amorous advances of a prefect who is passing by.[34] Of the three adaptations of this tale in women's script, one is a fragment, and the most detailed version (in the handwriting of Gao Yinxian) breaks off shortly before the conclusion, so the brief version translated in chapter 7 is the transcription by Yi Nianhua.[35]

Lu Qiuhu is the single son of a family so rich that "even a bird cannot fly across all their fields." He is married to lady Luo, but on the fourth day of their married life, he takes his leave in order to pursue an official career. After nine years, a dream implies that his father has died and thereby urges him to return home. Outside his home village, he encounters a pretty woman picking mulberry leaves. He proposes to her, offering her gold and silver and silks if she accepts, but she indignantly refuses his offer. He proceeds to his house, where they meet again. When lady Luo realizes that the scoundrel who tried to seduce her is actually her husband, she retires to her room, takes leave of her possessions, and drowns herself in a river. The more extensive version of the tale ends in the middle of a scene set at Qiuhu's parental home. Qiuhu visits lady Luo in her room in order to thank her for taking care of his parents, but she berates him for trying to seduce her, and the final lines read: "You were serious when you tried to seduce me / But I never had any desire to react."[36]

One can only assume that in this version of the story, the original also would end in her suicide.

Perhaps the best-known tale in traditional China about a wife's fidelity to her absent husband is the story of Meng Jiangnü.[37] Meng Jiangnü does not stay at home, waiting for her husband's return, but takes the unprecedented step of traveling all by herself, far from home, to the Great Wall. The outline of this legend was already established during the Tang dynasty (617–906), but its sources may in turn be traced back to pre-Han times, to the tale of the wife of Qi Liang, who brought down a wall with her crying.[38] Meng Jiangnü marries a young man (Fan Qilang) who is hiding in the garden of her parents' home and happens to see her in the nude while she is bathing in the garden pond. The young man is a conscript laborer who had fled the hard labor of construction on the Great Wall, and following the marriage, he returns to his assigned work site. There he quickly dies of exhaustion, and his remains are buried in the Great Wall. Meanwhile, Meng Jiangnü has been preparing a set of winter clothes for her husband. She travels to the Great Wall in order to deliver them, but when she arrives, she finds out he has died. She weeps until the Great Wall collapses at the spot where he had been buried and identifies his bones by dropping some of her blood on them.

In the course of centuries, this tale knew many variations. Some versions elaborate on Meng Jiangnü's miraculous birth, others develop her adventures while traveling from her hometown to the Great Wall, and yet others allow a major part to the cruel First Emperor, who seeks to marry this virtuous widow. Other versions of the legend focus only on major episodes from the tale.[39] Among the songbook adaptations, two manuscripts in women's script treat these materials: a shorter version by Yi Nianhua alone and a longer version, prepared by Yi Nianhua in 1986 in cooperation with the cultural worker Zhou Shuoyi. Both versions are titled *Meng Jiangnü*. The shorter version of the legend focuses on three episodes in the story: Meng Jiangnü's demand that Fan Qilang marry her after he has observed her taking a bath; Fan Qilang's forced departure for the Great Wall during their wedding night; and her longing for her absent husband during each of the twelve months of the year. The longer version, which appears to be based on another original, covers the same episodes but at more length; it includes an extended introduction and a summary account of Meng Jiangnü's trip to the Great Wall, where she learns about her husband's death.[40] Translations of both the shorter and the longer version of the tale are in chapter 8, "The Maiden Meng Jiang."

As it is, few peasant women will have suffered the long absence of a husband who was pursuing an official career. However, a prolonged absence due to trading trips, employment outside the home village, and the military draft was a common occurrence. Moreover, as the lines quoted above demonstrate, the theme of fidelity to an absent husband is closely related to the theme of a widow's loyalty to her deceased husband. Traditional morality has often been attacked for its prohibition of a widow's remarriage, which has been decried as a denial of a woman's sexual and emotional needs. The literature in women's script, however, shows Jiangyong women to be staunch supporters of this ban on remarriage. Many autobiographical ballads stress the sufferings their authors endured in order to remain loyal to their deceased husbands and raise their children. These autobiographical ballads also offer evidence supporting the findings of many anthropologists that a woman in traditional China could ensure her social security only if she bore a successor to her husband's family and had a son on whom to rely. A number of autobiographical ballads tell the sorry fate of widows who were urged to remarry after 1949 but were unceremoniously turned out by the children of their second husbands' first wives as soon as the second husbands died; at the same time, these women's children by their first husbands also were not eager to take their mothers in.

ENDANGERED REPUTATIONS

Two of the women's script manuscripts are adaptations of ballads treating stories from the corpus of Judge Bao's judicial cases.[41] The character of Judge Bao is based on the historical official Bao Zheng (999–1062), who established a reputation as an astute and incorruptible judge, willing to stand up to even the most powerful men (and women) in the land in order to see justice done. The cases of Judge Bao were adapted as plays and ballads from at least as early as the fourteenth century and have remained popular with Chinese audiences to this very day. These two stories transcribed in women's script share the common theme of female chastity: in the first case, a married woman is threatened with rape but resists, and in the second case, an unmarried woman is unjustly accused of premarital sexual activity and takes steps to safeguard her reputation. Both stories detail some of the dangers to which a woman exposes herself by leaving the confines of the inner quarters and exposing herself to the gaze of others, a topic also mentioned in the adaptation of the Meng Jiangnü tale. In both stories, however, the female heroine is anything but a passive victim of fate, as both women show initiative, courage, and independence of action.

The longest text by far is chapter 9, "The Flower Seller" (Maihuanü). This is one of the longest texts among the songbook adaptations. As the original transcription was made by Hu Cizhu, the women's script adaptation must have been made before 1976, the year of her death. This story takes place in Kaifeng during the reign of Emperor Renzong (r. 1022–62) and tells the tale of Liu Sijun and his wife, lady Zhang. Liu Sijun is the sole survivor of a once very rich family that is now pursued by disaster. When the family has been reduced to such poverty that they are living outside town in a dilapidated kiln, lady Zhang decides to make some money for her husband and baby son by selling paper flowers. She persists in this intention despite her husband's protests.

When she enters town, she is warned by an old man, an incarnation of the Taibai star (who frequently appears in these texts), not to sell flowers around the mansion of the emperor's father-in-law, Cao, but she ignores his warning. Cao notices her, takes a fancy to her, and calls her inside, where he proposes that she become one of his concubines. She refuses, despite his threats. Cao thereupon has her beaten to death and buried in his flower garden.

The soul of lady Zhang then appears to her husband in a dream, informs him of the manner of her death, and instructs him to appeal to the prefect of Kaifeng, Judge Bao. When Liu Sijun goes into town and runs into an official cortege, he immediately appeals to the official, who turns out to be none other than Cao, who, afraid of the ghost of lady Zhang, is on his way to a temple in order to burn incense. Cao has Liu Sijun arrested and locked up in his own mansion.

The soul of lady Zhang now appeals directly to Judge Bao, informing him of the spot where she has been buried. Judge Bao immediately invites himself to a flower-viewing party at Cao's and, once there, tells Cao that he had a dream about a treasure hoard buried in the garden that he will share with Cao. When Judge Bao's underlings start digging, they discover the corpse of lady Zhang. The judge immediately has Cao arrested and Liu Sijun set free. When the empress herself visits Judge Bao to intercede on behalf of her father, Judge Bao has Cao beheaded without further ado. He next restores lady Zhang to life. The empress appeals to Emperor Renzong and demands the lives of Liu Sijun and lady Zhang in repayment for the life of her father, and Judge Bao protests. The emperor sides with Judge Bao and awards official titles to both Liu Sijun and his wife.[42]

Chapter 10, "The Demonic Carp" (Liyujing), is a second, much shorter Judge Bao tale. In it, a carp takes on the shape of a girl and visits a young man in his study at night. The beautiful phantom drops a hairpin, which his parents later recognize as one of the betrothal gifts they had sent to the boy's bride-to-be. Scandalized by the behavior of their son's fiancée, they want to call off the engagement, and the indignant girl insists on appealing to Judge Bao. Using his magic mirror, Judge Bao quickly identifies and punishes the real culprit, clearing the girl's name.[43]

Judge Bao plays a very important role in the first story, but his role in the second tale is very limited indeed. In both stories, the heroines occupy center stage. In "The Flower Seller," lady Zhang takes the initiative when her husband is unable to provide for their family; she defends her honor even at the cost of her own life and, once dead, does not rest until she has been vindicated. It may only be poetic justice, but it still seems logical that such a strong-minded woman is allowed to come back to life. Her weak and foolish husband is a perfect foil for her strong and independent character: as soon as she entrusts him with a task, he bungles it by appealing to the first official in sight without ascertaining his identity. Lady Zhang has her counterpart in Empress Cao. Whereas lady Zhang puts her husband's family first and is willing to sacrifice her own life for the sake of chastity, Empress Cao ignores morality in her loyalty to her family of birth.

Anne McLaren has compared "The Flower Seller" to a ballad from the second half of the fifteenth century with an almost identical plot, "Judge Bao Solves the Case of Imperial Clansman Cao" (Bao Longtu duan Cao guojiu zhuan). In the fifteenth-century ballad, it is Judge Bao who is the center of attention. Lady Zhang comes to the capital only to accompany her husband, who will sit for the civil-service examinations, and it is the restless spirit of her murdered husband who alerts Judge Bao to the crime. Anne McLaren therefore concludes, "In the *nüshu* rendition, Wife Zhang's activities as a seller of flowers and later as an aggrieved ghost put her at the center of the narrative from beginning to end." She also states, "A tale focusing on the cunning of Judge Bao is retold as the tale of an aggrieved female ghost seeking justice."[44] However, we are not allowed to conclude that the women of Jiangyong introduced this change as they transliterated their source, because the women's script version shares this emphasis on lady Zhang with some other local adaptations of these materials.

As for "The Demonic Carp," in one alternative version of the story, the parents of the wronged girl take the initiative in appealing to Judge Bao, whereas in the women's script adaptation, it is the girl who insists on clearing her name of the socially deadly imputation of unchastity. In this respect, it may be pointed out that one of the original songs in women's script concerns the sad fate of a girl who is raped, takes to her bed as soon as she gets home, and dies within a few days.[45] McLaren further concludes from her comparison and related studies that "for *nüshu* women, chastity is a matter of upholding the primary relationship, that between the married couple, rather than exemplary loyalty to the mother-in-law. Women may be inferior and polluted but they have the power to demand fidelity from departing husbands and have a vested interest in the filial piety of their sons."[46]

QUESTIONING GENDER NORMS

The texts discussed so far show the women of Jiangyong as staunch upholders of traditional morality as far as matters of fidelity and chastity are concerned.[47] This does not mean that they were unaware of the iniquity of traditional gender norms as codified in the marriage system. In a number of Third-Day Letters, the system's arbitrariness and unfairness are decried but are also taken for granted. Among the adaptations of songbook texts in women's script, there are, moreover, a number of stories that may be read at one level as inquiries into gender norms and the possibility of change. These stories are the tragic romance of Liang Shanbo and Zhu Yingtai and the pious legend of Fifth Daughter Wang. Both stories were, and still are, widely popular in China.[48] The first, about Liang Shanbo and Zhu Yingtai, can be traced back at least to the Song dynasty (960–1278), and the latter, about Fifth Daughter Wang, is first encountered in sixteenth-century sources. The tale of Liang Shanbo and Zhu Yingtai was popular in Jiangyong, as demonstrated by the two versions in women's script (one a short fragment), and the tale of Fifth Daughter Wang had been adapted into women's script by Hu Cizhu, that is, before 1976.[49]

The tale of Liang Shanbo and Zhu Yingtai, transcribed by Gao Yinxian and translated in chapter 11, "The Karmic Affinity of Liang and Zhu" (Liang Zhu yinyuan), does not depart widely from one of its well-known versions. Zhu Yingtai, the real protagonist of the tale, is a girl who scandalizes her family by demanding that she be allowed to leave home in order to study in an academy.[50] Eventually, when she has been able to trick even her father with her male disguise, her parents give in to her insistent request. Once she has set out, dressed as a student, on her journey to a school, she meets Liang Shanbo, a young man from the same town, who is traveling for the same purpose. Together they trek to Hangzhou, where they enroll in an academy and share a room.

Every time Liang Shanbo suspects that his roommate may be a girl because she refuses to undress, because she urinates in a squatting position, or because she has large nipples, she succeeds in convincing him that she really is a boy. However, when their teacher orders all the students to take their summer baths, Zhu Yingtai realizes that the game is up and suddenly decides to leave for home. As she has fallen in love with her roommate in the meantime, she repeatedly attempts to suggest to him her true sex and her feelings while he is seeing her off, but he does not understand even the most obvious hints. She tells him to visit her parents and ask for her "younger sister" in marriage, but only after Liang Shanbo has returned to the academy does he find out about the true state of affairs.

By the time Liang Shanbo visits the Zhus, however, Zhu Yingtai's father has already promised her in marriage to the son of a rich and powerful local family, the Mas. Liang returns home, falls sick, and dies for love. On the day of her wedding, Zhu Yingtai asks that her sedan chair be taken past his grave. When she arrives there, thunder crashes, rain pours down, and the grave opens wide. She jumps into its gaping mouth, and the grave mound closes over her. The souls of the lovers are transformed, in this version, into a couple of mandarin ducks (not into the more usual butterflies).[51]

The tale of Liang Shanbo and Zhu Yingtai demonstrates the fate of a girl who tries to participate in male society: she may dress up as a male, and even fool most of the men most of the time, but eventually her body will tell on her.[52] As soon as her naked body is exposed to the male gaze, she will be fixed forever in her role as woman. Gender norms are based on physical differences that a disguise hides only temporarily. Zhu Yingtai's very attempt to overstep the boundaries imposed by her gender will be her undoing. She compounds her problems by falling in love with her roommate, acknowledging, not repressing, her body and its sexual desire. In modern times, the romance of Liang Shanbo and Zhu Yingtai has often been read as a feminist manifesto, condemning the traditional marriage system and calling for education for women. By demanding to be allowed to study, Zhu Yingtai insists on participating on an equal footing in the defining activity of elite male existence, breaking down the ultimate male privilege of traditional Chinese society. In such a reading, the twentieth century, with its successful implementation of coeducation and reform of the marriage system, may be hailed as the fulfillment of the tale's underlying demands. I, however, would rather see it as a narrative demonstration of the impossibility of wishful thinking.

The only possible way for a woman to escape her gender held out by these ballads is to follow a different course altogether. It requires a lifetime of devout recitation of Buddhist sutras and a total negation of the body and its sexuality, which, as shown in the tale of Fifth Daughter Wang, may result in rebirth as a male. The tale of Fifth Daughter Wang is traced back to at least the sixteenth century. A performance by nuns of this tale in the form of a "precious scroll" (baojuan) is described in the sixteenth-century novel *Plum in the Golden Vase* (Jin ping mei). The later development of this tale in northern and southern China has been extensively studied by Beata Grant.[53] The tale's widespread popularity in China to this very day is also demonstrated by the novel *The Butcher's Wife* (Shafu), by the Taiwanese female novelist Li Ang, which may be read as a realistic inversion of the tale of Fifth Daughter Wang.

According to the songbook version in chapter 12, transcribed by Hu Cizhu and titled simply "Fifth Daughter Wang" (Wang Wuniang), the heroine is a most pious girl from the moment of her birth. She does not eat meat, and her greatest pleasure is to recite the Diamond Sutra. When she reaches marriageable age, her parents marry her off to a certain Zhao Lingfang, with whom she bears two children, a boy and a girl. Zhao Lingfang is a butcher, who makes a living by slaughtering pigs, and he demands that his wife prepare the boiling water for scalding the slaughtered animals. When Fifth Daughter Wang urges her husband to give up this sinful way of life, he answers that his family has prospered for generations in this business, that he doesn't care about unfounded theories of karmic retribution, and that she, as a woman, is much more sinful than he anyway, because she soils the earth and all the gods in the house and the universe every time she sheds blood in giving birth or menstruating. Fifth Daughter Wang is stunned by the revelation of this paradox, that she sins by giving birth, and insists on living apart from her husband from that very moment. He accedes to her request when she answers all his questions on the Diamond Sutra correctly.

The exceptional piety of Fifth Daughter Wang even upsets King Yama, who decides to summon her to the underworld, so he may test her knowledge of the Diamond Sutra. The four messengers of death summon Fifth Daughter to the underworld, and she takes her leave of her husband and children. Before she dies, she writes her name on her calf, and the messengers take her to the world below. While others, sinners all, suffer many kinds of cruel punishments for the crimes they committed during their lives, Fifth Daughter Wang passes all the danger spots safely and proceeds through the ten courts of hell without a hitch. Whenever there is a problem, she solves it by reciting a few lines of the Diamond Sutra. Her early death is explained by the fact that she had once unintentionally damaged a paper copy of the Diamond Sutra, and she is allowed to be reborn as a man. Fifth Daughter requests rebirth as a Chinese, and not as a foreigner, and as a palanquin carrier so that she will have to commit no sin in the course of her daily work. It is decided, however, that she will be reborn as the only son of a rich and pious family.

Reborn as the son of the Zhang family, Fifth Daughter shows herself to be a bright student, who passes all the examinations in quick succession and even achieves top-of-the-list status. She thereupon requests the emperor to appoint her prefect of the prefecture where Zhao Lingfang and her children live. As soon as she arrives, she summons her husband and children, identifies herself to them by showing the inscription on her calf, quits her office, and devotes the rest of her life to religious exercises, joined by her husband and children. Eventually, the Jade Emperor sends them all to the Western Paradise while dragons build a palace for them in the ocean.[54]

Even this brief summary makes clear the reasons this legend held such appeal for Chinese women, in Jiangyong and elsewhere. It provided them with a concrete method for escaping from their female condition and even held out the reward of top-of-the-list status. While Zhu Yingtai failed to secure gender equality by intruding aggressively into the male domain and submitting to desire, Fifth Daughter Wang eventually outperformed all men by her rejection of society and its values and her total denial of sexuality. Although the legend stresses the efficacy of the recitation of the Diamond Sutra, it proclaims its nondenominational and universal nature by joining the Jade Emperor and the Western Paradise in the final lines of its text.

At the same time, the legend of Fifth Daughter Wang is the mirror image of yet another master narrative of traditional China, the legend of the monk Mulian. This legend was well known in Jiangyong, and the women's script texts refer to it a number of times. Both legends satisfy curiosity about the underworld with their extensive and detailed descriptions of the realm of King Yama and the procedures followed there. But the Mulian legend was a male narrative and was habitually performed as community drama in public spaces. The legend stresses, in whatever version one reads, the sinful nature of women, and every performance of the legend of Mulian therefore is also a public affirmation of male dominance by the patriarchal community. The only man who can save woman, the legend declares, is the man who has freed himself of any lingering attachment to women, even his mother, by leaving the family.

In the south, the story of Fifth Daughter Wang never enjoyed much popularity on the stage (dramatic adaptations in northern China focus on her misadventures before her marriage, when her wicked stepmother wants to couple Fifth Daughter to her good-for-nothing son). The story of Fifth Daughter Wang spread primarily in the form of ballads, we may assume, in the more private sphere of women's groups, as it was very much a female narrative. Whereas Mulian was a son who saved his sinful mother from hell as a filial monk, Fifth Daughter Wang was a wife who was able to rescue her sinful husband and her children from a comparable fate by fulfilling, and negating, her sexuality and fertility. Women, even mothers, were sinners to be saved in the Mulian legend, but in the legend of Fifth Daughter Wang, the woman becomes the savior of the family, including even its sinful men.

CONCLUSION

The versified moral tracts and narrative ballads selected by the women of Jiangyong for transliteration into women's script offer us a unique window into the mentality of traditional peasant women. Together, these texts offer a coherent picture of a demanding code of values that called for a life of thrift and diligence and for perseverance in the face of pain and disappointment. The ballads, moreover, insist on loyalty to one's husband despite poverty and long periods of absence as well as chastity after his death. The ballads also spell out the dangers for women of leaving the inner quarters but also show that taking on the trappings of the male gender offers no solution to the restrictions of the female condition—only a life of piety holds out the promise of rebirth as a man. Even if these ballads do not offer the excitement of warfare and conquest portrayed in epics that revolve around male heroes, they demand from their female audience the same if not a greater fortitude, and so they may well qualify as epics for women.

PART I

MORAL TRACTS

1

ADMONITIONS FOR MY DAUGHTER

Edited by Zhou Shuoyi

Nights are short during the hot days of the Sixth Month;
By the light of a lamp I was busy with my needlework,
While my darling daughter took a fully-rounded fan
And chased fireflies in front of the hall and behind it.
    I put down needle and thread and called my daughter:
"Please listen to me as I will explain a few things.
    When I was a girl in my mother's house, I remember,
I would wait on her day and night in the high hall.
And at that time your grandmother, that is my mother,
Would instruct all her children in their duties and tasks.
    Getting up early in the morning, I did my needlework,
And late at night, with no one around, I recited my texts,
But because my memory was not very good at all,
I often would promptly forget what I had just read.
    But my mother would never take me to task for this;
She would only teach me to recognize the radicals.[1]
But in the event my needlework was not up to standards,
She'd berate me in such a way that I really felt ashamed.
    She'd say, 'My daughter, you still may be very young,
But you have to think carefully in everything you do.

When reading books, the issue is to grasp the meaning;
There's no need to write poems and compose essays.
You have to apply yourself to twisting and spinning,
Only so your boxes will be filled with cloth and linens.

No matter whether it is freezing cold or night or day,
You have to fully taste sweet, sour, bitter, and hot.
Even though wealth and poverty may depend on fate,
Devotion to hard work is still the constant norm.

In ancient times there lived a woman called Jing Jiang
Who spent all her life, till her dying day, spinning thread.
The Master Confucius held her up to us all as a model:
Each and every one should imitate this woman Jing Jiang.²

You, my darling daughter, today still are very young,
But you are not allowed to neglect your needlework!

I also again and again have heard people explain
That a woman should dress herself most properly.
One's character depends on virtue, not on beauty,
So do not compete with others in following fashion.

I hope that you will carefully remember all this
And from now on will try to be good at all times.
There's no need to discuss what has happened before,
But don't ever let your mother down from now on!'

Deep in my heart I still remember each and every line
Of the advice I received from my mother in those days.
Since then, all my life I've never been able to forget;
Late at night I quite often still think of my mother.

In the blink of an eye now twenty years have passed,
And suddenly I find myself here as your mother.
So now I've told you everything from the beginning,
And I hope that you have listened with understanding.

I want you not to abandon yourself to play again
But to devote yourself to spinning and weaving.
When I now remember your grandmother, my mother,
Tears course down my cheeks and wet my gown—

Who could have known that it would already be so late?
Look, the moon sinking in the west, lighting up the wall."

2

THE TEN MONTHS OF PREGNANCY

Collected and edited by Zhou Shuoyi

Please allow me to tell you a few simple lines:
As human beings we must repay our parents' favors.
If you do not repay the favors done by your parents,
You will live your life here on earth all in vain!

This book does not deal with any other matter;
It narrates only all the sufferings of pregnancy.

Pregnant in the First Month, the first of the First:
It has no form, it has no shape, it makes no sound.
It looks like a leaf of watercress on the water—
Will it take root or not when all is said and done?

Pregnant in the Second Month with its bright sky:
This is when the embryo really mounts the body.
Your legs feel weak, you don't want to walk much;
Your arms feel weak, no love for needlework now!

Pregnant in the Third Month, the third of the Third:
Of the three meals a day, you will eat only two.
You don't care for tea, and you don't care for rice;
You want only sour bayberries and sour soup.

Pregnant in the Fourth Month, as it starts to show:
You're feeling pain all over and find it hard to walk.

That may be a minor matter when you are young,
But when you're pregnant at a later age, it's no fun!
  Pregnant in the Fifth Month, with its Double-Five:[1]
Oh my, to be heavy with child really is quite a pain!
Had I known that being pregnant was such suffering,
I'd rather have shaved my hair and entered a nunnery!
  Pregnant in the Sixth Month, the dog days of summer:
Burning incense and paper money, you pray to the gods.
I hope that you numinous gods will take pity on me
And will safely protect me when I go into labor.
  Pregnant in the Seventh Month, the time of harvest:
The whole family is busy at home and in the fields.
Cutting firewood for cooking—up the ridge in sorrow;
Carrying water for washing—down the slope in sorrow.
  Pregnant in the Eighth Month, autumn winds chilly:
My husband is all taken up in the transport of grain.
Don't take long trading trips to faraway places and
Quickly come home from trading trips not too distant!
  Pregnant in the Ninth Month, your belly a balloon:
There are all those many things you can't do anymore.
In your heart you long to go back to your mother's place,
But then you're afraid your son may be born on the road.
  Pregnant in the Tenth Month, the baby about to be born:
That child in your belly now is oh so heavy a load!
Your arms are so weak, and your legs are all swollen,
And each and every activity has become a burden.

Even more so once the contractions in your belly start:
Only a sheet of paper separates you from King Yama![2]
Each contraction is such pain that with each you die;
Two contractions are such pain that you lose your soul.
  Clenching your teeth, you could bite an iron nail in two;
Your arms and legs feel like ice being added to snow.
And even if the child is born easily, without a hitch,
The mother's life still very much hangs in the balance.

When my child falls to the ground and cries once,
My parents-in-law in the hall finally feel at ease.

When my child falls to the ground and cries twice,
The mother in her room opens her eyes wide.
    When my child falls to the ground and cries thrice,
People look closely to see whether it is a boy or a girl.
A foot-washing basin is filled to wash his body;
I hold my baby, wrapped in a silk skirt, in my arms!

The happy news is reported to its grandmother;[3]
They kill a rooster for her to repay her for her grace.
    When the grandmother hears this, she's filled with joy:
"My daughter finally has given me a grandchild!"
She grabs a chicken, and she also brings eggs;
She doesn't wait to change into some new clothes.
    A good day is chosen to celebrate the Third Day,[4]
And baskets and packets are piled up together.
All the way on the road she is beaming with joy,
And, talking and laughing, she arrives at the gate.
    Seeing her, the parents-in-law are filled with joy;
They invite the grandmother to come inside.
They invite her to take the seat of honor,
And the Third Day is celebrated with great ado.

Let's leave aside the Third Day and not discuss it;
Let's talk again about the mother and her child.
    At the age of one and two he drinks his mother's milk;
At the age of two and three he never leaves her side.
At the age of five and six he then learns to talk;
At the age of seven and eight he reads the books.
    Paper and ink, brush and inkstone are all provided;
All effort is made to teach her son to read the books.
    And when her son leaves the house to read his books,
His mother, sitting in her room, waits for his return.
From the early dawn when he left, she waits till noon,
And from noon she waits till his return at nightfall.
    Firstly she fears that her son may suffer some cold;
Secondly she fears because her son is still so young;
Thirdly she fears that her son may climb into a tree;

Fourthly she fears that her son may walk to the river.

Fifthly she fears that her son may attract some illness;
Sixthly she fears that her son may suffer an empty fright;[5]
Seventhly she fears that her son may develop smallpox;
Eighthly she fears that her son may not live to grow up.

Ninthly she fears that her son may not have the talent;
Tenthly she fears that her son may not form a family.
Each day she waits, hoping her son will turn into a man,
Will grow up into a man and have a marriage partner.

When she has raised her son to the age of eighteen or so,
She finds him a wife to settle him for the rest of his life.
When the wife he has married turns out to be wise,
His father and mother also can put their minds at ease.

One hopes that one's son and his wife will be filial,
So flowers will bloom again, the moon be full again!
If you respect your father and mother for four ounces,
Your own son and heir will show you half a pound.

Those who are filial will have sons who are filial;
Disobedient sons will be fathers of disobedient children.
If you don't believe us, look at the water from the roof:
Each and every drop drips down on the same spot!

If you are not filial, that may be only a minor matter,
But if your son is not filial to you, it wounds your heart.
If you raise a boy, he'll not know his mother's hardship;
If you raise a daughter, she'll repay her parents' favors.

Let's leave aside this subject and not discuss it, but
Let's go back and again describe a mother's mind.

If her son wets the bed on one side, he sleeps on the other,[6]
While his mother moves from the dry spot to the wet spot.
And if he has wetted both sides through and through,
She holds him in her arms all night, till break of day!

In one day he drinks three bellyfuls of his mother's milk;
In three days he drinks nine bellyfuls of his mother's milk.

A mother's milk is not the water of the Long River;
It is not the roots of ferns and bushes on the hills:

Each and every mouthful he drinks is his mother's blood!
Because of his drinking, his mother's skin turns sallow.

Let's not talk of the hardships of the child's father—
A mother spends all her energy in raising her son.
The sufferings of pregnancy cannot be fully narrated,
So sons and daughters should never forget this favor.
    Each of you in turn will become a father or a mother,
So please teach your children to remember this well!

3

THE FAMILY HEIRLOOM

Written᠎ out᠎ by Gao Yinxian᠎

Please allow me to tell you a few simple lines:
As human beings we must repay our parents' favors.
If you do not repay the favors shown by your parents,
You will live your life here on earth all in vain!

From the very moment the mother is pregnant,
She is never at ease, whether sitting or sleeping.
She loses all taste for food, her skin turns sallow—
Painful breathing, swollen legs, and a dizzy head!
    The mother should not walk up or down steep roads;
When she walks, she is careful because of that life.
While the mother is already secretly filled with fear,
The father, unbeknownst to her, is sick with worry.
    Through a thousand sufferings she brings it to term;
Only after ten months of pregnancy she gives birth.
    In case anything goes wrong during the baby's birth,
Father and mother, awash in tears, fear for its life!
The mother calls on the gods; the father makes a vow,
Praying to the gods to protect the safety of wife and son.
    The pangs of pain in her belly feel like knife cuts;

She swoons repeatedly and regains consciousness;
She is separated from King Yama by one sheet of paper.
The father kowtows to the house gods in front of the hall.
    Even when the child, boy or girl, has been born,
The life of the mother still hangs in the balance.
Whether it is a boy or a girl, she's filled with joy,
While the father thanks the gods in front of the hall.

The mother considers the child like a treasure;
The father considers the child like a pile of gold.
The boy sleeps in a dry spot, the mother in his pee,
Not daring to make any move, afraid to scare him.
    In case the child suffers from any kind of disease,
The mother is flustered and worried and cannot sleep.
The fathers hurries to call a doctor to treat the baby;
The mother makes vows and also prays to the gods.
    Only when the child has recovered from the disease,
Can the father and mother be at ease again and relax.
    Then they worry that the parents' fate may be evil,
So they entrust it to other parents, change its name.[1]
They don't care how much money they have to spend,
As they want to make sure their son lives to grow up.
    Then they always worry that the boy suffers hunger and cold,
That his mother's milk is not enough to boost his body.
His hands are always filled with cakes and candies—
Still they worry about water and fire and idle snacks.
    His playing in high and low places worries his mother;
His running around all over the place upsets his father.
When eventually he reaches the age of six or seven,
His father and mother have really worn out their hearts!

By this time they send their son to school, as they hope
That he'll become a good person by reading the books.
Sun and moon are like a shuttle, passing oh so quickly,
And at the age of sixteen or seventeen he's grown up!
    Even though he may not yet have achieved fame through study,
The proper time for a marriage now quickly approaches.

They ask a matchmaker to look for a virtuous daughter
Who will be a willing marriage partner for their son.
    For the selected day they buy meat of pigs and goats,[2]
A most lavish banquet, and then the engagement gifts.
The rich will invite their guests for three or five days;
Even those who are poor will still invite their relatives.
    New clothes and a red sedan chair are all provided—
It takes his father and mother endless care and worry!

Bringing home a daughter-in-law, one is filled with joy;
People all tell you that from now on, you will be served!
If the son is aware of all the hardships of his parents,
His wife, too, is bound to obey his parents most filially.
    But, alas, there also are sons who are good-for-nothings:
Once they have married, they change their hearts.
Husband and wife live in harmony like fish and water,
And he doesn't give any thought to his dear parents.
    When his wife goes to her mother's home, he also goes,
And as long as his wife doesn't return, he doesn't either.[3]
He goes and lives in the house of his father-in-law and
Only rarely returns home to his own family.
    He only wants to have a wonderful time with his wife
And now treats his own father and mother like strangers.
When he does return home and his parents berate him,
He'll answer his father and mother in words most foul.
    But when his wife has words with him and berates him,
He will hasten to make her smile by making amends.

When there is work to do and you tell him to do it,
He will holler and scream and demand a division.
If he doesn't say his elder brother has too many kids,
He will say that his father and mother are too partial.
    His wife will holler and scream and feign a suicide,
And your son will grab a knife, threatening murder.
The father and mother fear that disaster may follow
And can do naught but agree to a division of the inheritance.
    The uncles on both sides of the family are invited,

And these many kinds of uncles come to the village.
The parents publicly divide the land and the fields;
Trees and treasure are divided according to share.
    When a list of the divided property has been drawn up
As proof, the sons and their wives are on their own.

There are all these many people, their own uncles,
Their aunts and their husbands, who all help out, but
They curse their uncles and aunts for their meddling,
And their father and mother feel very unpleasant.
    But what they find out is truly most unbearable:
The brothers divide the months to feed their parents.
There's no idea of helping the parents live their lives;
They complain that elderly people are hard to please.
    The son says one word and his wife says another, and
They end up complaining they're feeding some idlers.
Alas, their elderly parents who suffered for half a life
Now may best be compared to men hoping for snow.[4]
    As the parents eat their portions of humiliating rice,
They'd like to die but can't, like to live but cannot.
The two parents are so upset that they would rather die
So as to lay a plaint before King Yama about their suffering.
    One raises sons, it is said, for one's care in old age—
Having no sons is better than having no life like this!

In case the father and mother suffer some illness,
They'll not see the son or his wife come to visit them,
And if friends and relatives come to visit them,
They will say that this is old age, like it should be.
    You'll not see your daughter-in-law bring some tea;
You'll not see your own son go and fetch a doctor.
They'll not keep you company, not come and look—
In vain you face the stillness of snow all by yourself.[5]

When his father and mother pass from this world,
He brings out a coffin and also buries the corpse.
His children and wife feign sadness and weep, but

Such weeping never yet brought a soul back to life.
       After three or five Sevens, the funeral takes place.[6]
That, they reckon, fully repays their parents' favors.
Then there are the rich who arrange home sacrifices,
And they invite priests and monks to recite the sutras.
       Offerings of pork and mutton may be on display,
But their father and mother never had a bite to eat.
They spend money in the name of honoring their parents,
But in the final analysis, it's a party thrown for relatives.
       All these many activities are only an empty show—
No match for proper care during your parents' lifetimes!
What's the use of a whole pig and goat as an offering?
Four ounces and pure broth, and we would be grateful!
       There's no need to weep your heart out when we die;
I just want you to have a filial heart while we're alive.

When the father and mother suffer a disastrous calamity,
The daughter-in-law and her children don't worry at all.
       [If they assisted their parents] when they have to visit the toilet[7]
And show care by keeping the fast and reciting sutras,
Then if their parents were to see this with their own eyes,
They'd be grateful, whatever divine help it might secure.

If we do not serve our father and mother most filially,
I'm afraid our sons and grandsons will do the same.
       Since ancient times good and evil have their retribution;
Heaven's eye observes it all, and no mercy is shown.
Those who are disobedient will have disobedient sons;
Those who are filial will in their turn have filial sons.
       In ancient times a certain Xiao Shu had three sons;
The retribution for good and evil was clear for all to see.
Cursing his father, the eldest son was struck by Thunder;[8]
His wife was burned to ashes because she was unfilial.
       The second son, who beat his mother, was pulverized;
His disobedient wife was devoured by hungry wolves.
The third son and his wife acted in a most filial way:
As a top of the list, he enjoyed the emperor's grace![9]

Meng Zong wept and prayed for bamboo shoots in winter;
Obeying his mother, he knelt down, without any arrogance.[10]
For his father's funeral Dong Yong sold himself as a slave,[11]
While Zhao Wuniang cut off her hair and offered it for sale.[12]
For all eternity the names of all these many men and women
Have been transmitted till today for their filial behavior!

Why on earth would I be a disobedient, rebellious person?
If I am not filial to my parents, it's because I don't know
How hurtful it is when my son does not serve me filially.
I only fear that when I will have grown old, be of no use,
My daughter-in-law will then do exactly the same to me.

4

THE LAZY WIFE

Collected and edited by Zhou Shuoyi

I will not tell about the Han, nor tell about the Tang,[1]
But listen, as I sing to you the story of the lazy wife.
All good elder and younger sisters, sitting all around,
Please listen very carefully as you sit by my side.

This girl had been pampered from her earliest years;
She spent her days too lazy to work but always eating;
When she turned eighteen and was married,
She drove her husband to distraction, drove him mad!
   When her husband told her to rise and get to work,
She feigned either a headache or a terrible cold,
But as soon as her husband left the house,
She jumped out of the bed, as if carried on a cloud.
   Three lumps of lean meat together with two eggs,
Brought up to taste with onions, pepper, and spices:
All alone she went on eating till she was stuffed,
Oblivious of the hunger and cold her husband suffered.

The rice she cooked for the three meals of the day
Was either still raw, or cooked to pulp, or full of water.

The vegetables she cooked were without any taste;
If they were not too bland, they were far too salty.
 If her husband wanted her to make him a pair of shoes,
She had no idea of foot or inch, and of long and short.
She'd make one that was long and one that was short;
She'd make one that was short and one that was long.
 And when her husband put them on his feet,
They were as hard and stiff as a buffalo's horn.

If relatives or friends invited her to a party,
She wanted to show off but didn't have the clothes.
 She'd try to borrow some from people all over the place,
But, alas, nobody paid any attention to her, as
Each and every one said that she was a lazy wife,
Too lazy by far to properly wash her own shirt and skirt.
 Her washing turned black into the hemp of mourning;[2]
Her washing turned white into chrysanthemum-yellow.
The front of her clothes was as rumpled as a tangerine;
The back of her clothes resembled a rumpled tangerine.
 Rumpled as a tangerine peel, a rumpled tangerine peel,
But rumpled as they might be, she still put them on.
And when she arrived at the house of her relatives,
Thousands of people in town collapsed in laughter!

When her relatives had set out the banquet,
She made sure she was seated in the best position.
When the host first served eggs cooked in noodles,
All the eggs would be gone in one flash of her chopsticks!
 With bulging eyes she selected the dishes to eat;
She would eat only dumplings and not drink any soup.
The host saw that she would not drink any wine,
As she'd drink only sweet wine, thrice-fermented brews.
 The host saw she would not eat any other dishes,
As she'd eat only dishes of chicken or fish or pork liver.
The host concluded that she would not eat any rice,
But three pints of white rice were just one meal.
 If the host put out ten separate dishes, she would
Not be happy until she had cleared off all these dishes!

When the banquet was finished, they sat together
And, with nothing else to do, chatted with one another.
Then someone would ask her the following question,
Would ask her what kind of work she was doing at home.

    "How much ramie did you twist into thread this year?
How many pounds of thread did you spin this one year?"
When they raised the issue of twisting and spinning,
She was dumbfounded, not saying a word, staring blankly.

    As she did not know very well how to speak back,
She promptly conceived of a different idea altogether.
Without wasting time on expressing thanks to the host,
She immediately hurried back home, all by herself.

    She traveled on and on, the entire road, walking very fast;
Because of her haste, her feet became covered with mud.
Once she arrived back home, she was all tired out
And did not give a damn about how muddy she might be.

    Once she fell down, she fell down on the cool bed
And did not give a damn about all the work in the house.
And if her husband cursed her out at that sight—
So just think what this woman's ending would be!

In this world every family has its own kind of daughters,
But a woman like this will create no end of troubles.
Dear sisters, please have a look for yourselves and say
Whether the story I told here is preposterous or not.

PART II

NARRATIVE BALLADS

5

THE TALE OF THIRD SISTER

Written out by Gao Yinxian

I have some sincere and earnest advice for you all:
Throughout your life never harbor any evil intentions!
If you deliberately harm others, you'll harm yourself:
In this world there's the court, beyond that the gods!

    As a man you should never use two kinds of bushels,
And as a woman never employ a duplicitous mind.
Don't measure what's coming in with a big bushel;
Don't measure what's going out with a small bushel.

    Thunder will strike those who use two bushels;
I'm afraid High Heaven will show no mercy at all!
Don't say that High Heaven acts without reason, as
The numinous gods hover three feet above your head.

    Once grown too old, the year's harvest can't be sold;
Do not add any grain gone bad to bushel and pint.
When you treat this precious grain like dirt and dust,
Your sons and grandsons will later not live in peace.

But let me not sing anymore of these idle words;
I will sing once again of the hardships of Third Sister.
This tale is not an event from some distant past but

43

A recent piece of news from the Guangxu period.[1]

Her family lived in Yongzhou Prefecture in Hunan;
Hers was a family within the Wang family compound.
Twenty miles to the east of the prefectural capital
Was a place that was called Wang Family Village.

The family of Mr. Wang was extremely wealthy;
The family owned more that five hundred good fields.
His wife was referred to by all as "old woman Wang";
She had given birth to one son and three daughters.

The one son stayed at home, as he studied the books,
And the three daughters all had been married off.

The eldest sister had been married to one of the Shous;
The second sister had been married to one of the Lis;
The third sister had been married to one of the Xiaos:
In this way the three daughters had all been married.

The eldest sister's family was immensely wealthy;
The second sister's family had lots of gold and silver.
It was only the third sister who suffered misfortune:
Once she arrived at the Xiaos, they were hit by poverty.

At the Xiao family they lacked the rice for tomorrow;
Third Sister did not have any good clothes to wear.
During daytime she felt cold in her unpadded clothes;
She was freezing [at night] with no blanket on the bed.

Her body was freezing and her stomach was empty, as
Each night she embroidered flowers till break of dawn.
How pitiable Third Sister who suffered such misfortune:
She met with a thousand kinds of hardship and bitter pain!

When woman Wang saw how her daughter was suffering,
She invited her back to her house and then said to her:
"It's all your parents' fault—we must have been blind!
We did not marry you to a rich family with lots of money!

We thought that the Xiao family was really well-to-do:
Who could have known that they are really dirt-poor?
This very moment they do not even have enough grain,
So this is the moment for you to marry someone else!

Now here on the street lives this young master Liu,

A smart and handsome fellow, sincere and honest, too!
Their grain fields are good for a few hundred loads,
And he is one of the students in the prefectural school.[2]

If you, my daughter, would marry into the Liu family,
You'd lead a life of luxury, glory, status, and wealth.
But if you, my daughter, don't marry someone new,
You will suffer hardship for all the years of your life."

Third Sister then addressed her mother as follows:
"My dear mother, please listen to what I have to say.

A good horse is not fitted out with a pair of saddles;
A good woman will not marry a second husband.
No one can ride on a horse with a pair of saddles;
A woman with two husbands ruins her reputation.

In my opinion, whatever happens to us is our fate,
As fixed by the eight characters and five elements.[3]
If each and every one wanted to be a high official,
Who would then be the official, and who the people?

Let others be a high official, let others be wealthy;
I love my bitter suffering, and I love my poverty.
My dear father and mother, please listen to me,
Please listen well to these examples from the past.

In ancient times there lived a man called Zhu Maichen;
His wife, detesting his poverty, married someone else.
Later in his life Zhu Maichen rose to riches and glory;
When his wife wanted to return, it could not be done.[4]

'Try to pick up the water I've spilled on the ground!'
For all eternity, throughout the ages, she is cursed.

But then you have the example of Lü Mengzheng:
Husband and wife lived together in an abandoned kiln,
But later his fortune took a turn: he passed the exams
With highest honors and became the top of the list.[5]

Xue Pinggui eventually became a Son of Heaven;
The wife he had been married to was Wang Baochuan.
She suffered hardship for eighteen years in an old kiln,
But later she attained the status of an imperial queen![6]

If this is the case with all these people from the past,
Why shouldn't this apply equally to your daughter, too?

Look how many poor people later ended up rich, and
How many wealthy people later ended up destitute!

You, my parents, may urge me to marry someone else,
But I will stick to the Xiao family till my dying day.
If you had married me to some other family,
It would be the same: I trust in fate and not in man.

Even though the Xiao family may be dirt-poor,
They treat me without any double-dealing at all.
But if I were now to decide to marry someone else,
I would deprive the Xiao family of all descendants."

Woman Wang answered her in the following words:
"My dear daughter, please listen to what I have to say.

My only wish is that you will live a life of luxury.
What do I care about their lack of descendants?
But if you, my daughter, refuse to obey your parents,
Don't blame your mother for what may go wrong!"

Upon hearing this, Third Sister was awash in tears.
"My dear smart mother, how considerate you are!

For what purpose was I born and raised by you?
Don't say your daughter didn't think this through.
If we had the choice to marry someone else,
Who would not want to become a well-to-do person?

After a thousand lives of virtue one shares a boat;
After a myriad lives of virtue one sleeps in one bed.
One night as a couple is a hundred nights of love;
A hundred nights as a couple—as deep as the ocean!

I, your daughter, am now sixteen years of age,
And I, too, now fully understand feeling and reason.
I've tasted sweet and sour, and bitter and astringent;
I never am able to sleep through the night till dawn.

I do not long for tender lamb and exquisite wines;
I dress myself in clothes made from coarse linen.
If King Yama has destined you for eight cups of rice,
Even at the end of the world it won't become ten.

If your fate holds it for you, you'll get it in the end;
If your fate doesn't have it, you only trouble your mind."

When woman Wang heard this, she loudly cursed her.

"My daughter, what you are saying makes no sense!
Husband and wife are just birds sharing a grove, and
When drought and famine come, each flies off alone.

Now you change your mind and give it some thought,
And we'll see whether you will marry someone else.
But if you continue to refuse to marry someone else,
Never again in all your life set foot in my house!"

Upon hearing this, Third Sister was awash in tears;
Tears coursed down her cheeks in great profusion.
Third Sister refused to do as her mother told her, so
She said good-bye to her parents and went back home.

Once she had gone one mile, there was another mile;
Once she had walked one stretch, there was another.
Continuing along her road, she quickly came home,
And soon she had arrived at the gate of the Xiaos.

As soon as her husband saw her, he asked the question,
"Third Sister, now allow me to ask you this question.
What matter did your parents want to discuss with you
When they invited you to come back to their place?"

Third Sister promptly answered him in these words:
"My dear husband, please listen to what I have to say.

The family of my eldest sister is extremely wealthy;
My second sister's family has lots of gold and silver.
But you and I, husband and wife, are truly miserable,
As it is a fact that here in this house we are dirt-poor.

As my father and mother see how destitute we are,
They urged me to leave you and marry someone else.
They want to marry me off to the Liu family, so I
May lead a life of luxury, glory, status, and wealth.

This is because my parents are bereft of all reason;
Preferring wealth over poverty, they want our divorce.
Now because I refused to obey my father and mother,
They promptly started to curse me, again and again:

If I would not marry that young master Liu, I was
Never again to set foot in my mother's house forever!
I considered all options and did not know what to do,

But as I love only my current life, I came back here.

I have thought all these things over in my own heart:
I'm happy to suffer and die here with the Xiao family.
Whatever we gain and whatever we lose, I'll stay here,
And I will never shrink from hard work and long toil.

I'll take my life as it comes, in good times and bad,
Even if it means I'll have to live in worry and care.
And if great wealth may indeed be a matter of fate,
Modest wealth depends on our will and our efforts.

And if Highest Heaven has eyes with which to see,
We later also may end up as people of great wealth!"

One day turned to three, and three then turned to nine,
And so they spent Double-Nine, the ninth of the Ninth.
With the Ninth Month gone, the Tenth Month arrived;
The weather turned colder, and they were ill prepared.

In the Twelfth Month snow fell down in wild profusion;
They were freezing [at night] with no blanket on the bed.
The hunger in their stomachs was still only a minor matter,
But having no clothes to wear—that hardship was terrible!

When the Last Month arrived, again one year had passed:
Husband and wife on this day were both awash in tears.
"Other people all have wine to celebrate the New Year,
But you and I have to enter the year without any wine!"

Third Sister promptly admonished her husband as follows:
"My dear husband, why do you have to cry without end?
Other people may have rice to celebrate the New Year,
But we will enter the New Year even without the rice."

Next door to them there lived an old woman Wang,
Who noticed how pitiable husband and wife truly were.
As a result, she not only measured out five cups of rice,
But she also gave half a pound of salt to Third Sister.

When she received this, Third Sister was quite happy:
"Many thanks, old lady, for all your generous gifts!
If later we are better off, we'll pay you back bit by bit,

As we are on both sides drinking from the same river."

Having brought the rice, woman Wang went back home.
But, alas, Third Sister still could not celebrate New Year!
She took the salt and sold four ounces of it on the street;
She took the rice and sold one cup of it on the street.

With the twenty or thirty copper coins she obtained,
She bought paper money and candles to thank the gods:
"May the numinous gods extend their protection to us;
May they protect us so our life may take a better turn!"

All of a sudden Third Sister's belly started to hurt,
As the baby boy in her belly was about to be born.

A piece of red silk was quickly placed on the ground;
When the baby was placed on the ground, he cried.
On the third day they selected a name for the baby;
The name they selected for him was Sanyuan.

Each day she spun thread till past midnight,
Her little baby boy all the while sitting on her knees.
As soon as her little baby boy started to cry,
She gave him her breast so he could drink.

And then Third Sister always told her son,
"My dear little baby, dear darling apple of my eye,
Your mother will raise you with greatest care, hoping
That life later will take a better turn for both of us."

In her heart Third Sister kept thinking [of her parents],
And these thoughts all of a sudden resulted in a dream.
"For years you have not returned to your mother's house;
Now a happy celebration is quickly approaching."

"My mother is indeed about to turn fifty-one, but how
Would I have the money to buy her a birthday present?"

Third Sister promptly called for her darling husband;
She repeatedly called for her husband, again and again.
Her husband promptly arrived and answered her, asking,
"My dear wife, for what reason are you calling me?"

"You are sleeping and snoring at ease in your bed,
But tomorrow a happy celebration is set to take place.

My mother will celebrate her birthday, turning fifty-one,
But how would I have the money to buy her a present?
   In this house we do not even have the rice for tomorrow,
And I do not even have half a copper cent in cash!"
   When her husband heard what his wife had to say,
He did not sleep at all that night, waiting for dawn.
And as soon as the earliest light appeared in the sky,
He took his ax for cutting wood and left for the hills.
   "You stay here with the baby and get some sleep,
While I will take off and make the trip to the hills."
   When he had cut a load of firewood, he sold it quickly;
By selling the firewood, he got forty copper coins,
And when he passed by the shop of the Wang family,
He bought with that money one pound of noodles.
   Carrying these noodles in both hands, he came home,
Where Third Sister welcomed him, her face one smile:
"While you stay here at home and do your work,
I will go and congratulate my mother on her birthday."
   Carrying that one pound of noodles in her left hand,
And with her baby on her back—off to her mother's place!
Walking on three-inch golden lotuses, she hurried on;[7]
All filled with happiness she made the trip home.

But let's not talk about Third Sister going back home;
Let's also talk about Eldest Sister and Second Sister.
   Eldest Sister had her boxes carried in one long row;
Second Sister had her boxes carried in proper order.
Eldest Sister followed behind, riding a sedan chair;
Second Sister followed behind, riding a sedan chair.
   Woman Wang welcomed them, all filled with joy,
And then had the presents carried in through the gate.
While these two sisters together entered the room,
Third Sister also arrived at the gate of the house.
   When the servant boy at the gate had gotten a look
And saw that Third Sister was coming back home,
He hurried inside to report to that old woman Wang,
"It is your third daughter who is coming back home!"

When woman Wang heard this, she was astounded.
"For years she hasn't come back to our house here!
Irrespective of the way she has her boxes carried
Have someone go and welcome her inside."

The servant boy thereupon answered as follows:
"I saw only Third Sister; she was all by herself.
In her left hand she carried one pound of noodles;
The little boy on her back must be your grandson."

When woman Wang heard this, she was angered
And ordered the servant boy to go and close the gate.
He promptly closed and locked the gate in front
Right when Third Sister arrived there at the gate.

Third Sister arrived at the gate [and wondered],
"Why have they suddenly closed the gate?"
In front of the gate she loudly called to be let in,
But no one inside the Wang family mansion reacted.

Third Sister pondered the situation in her heart,
Then turned around and went to the back gate.
When Third Sister so appeared in the high hall,
Her mother cursed her loudly once she saw her.

"I told you a long time ago to marry someone else,
But you refused to marry a rich man with money!
Eldest Sister is wearing clothes of gauze and silk;
Second Sister is wearing gold and silver jewelry.

But I only have to take one look at you to see
Your clothes have been patched, and patched again.
You've come here to put your parents to shame,
Not to offer me your birthday congratulations!"

This day the guests were many, quite a crowd,
So her mother could not fully display her meanness.
So her mother immediately ordered Third Sister
To go and stay in the kitchen, tending the fire.

"The weather is cold and your clothes are unpadded,
So you'd better go and tend the fire in the kitchen."
The guests in the hall were all treated to dinner,
To the loudly resounding music of pipes and drums.

Relatives and friends all were given places to sit,
But Third Sister was kept busy tending the fire.

The grandmother carried her grandson in her arms;
Carrying her grandson, she came into the kitchen.
She selected a chicken leg and gave it to the boy,
And the son of Eldest Sister then stopped crying.
    The son of Second Sister wept most piteously, so
The grandmother carried this grandson in her arms.
She also selected a nice chicken leg for this boy,
And the son of Second Sister then stopped crying.
    The son of Third Sister also wept most piteously;
His grandmother also carried him in her arms and,
Feigning love, also came with him to the kitchen.
    But she didn't select anything nice for him to eat;
All she got the little boy was an old radish.
Third Sister's little boy felt the pangs of hunger,
So he took the radish and swallowed it whole!
    When woman Wang saw this, she was angered
And took out a stick to give her grandson a beating,
Cursing him for being no better than a beggar
Who would come to nothing but poverty and hunger.
    When Third Sister saw this, she spoke as follows:
"Mother, now please listen to what I have to say.
To Eldest Sister's little boy you gave a chicken leg;
To Second Sister's little boy you gave exactly the same.
    But my little son, who already has such a bitter fate,
All you gave him was only this one old radish!
Palm or backside of the hand—both your own flesh:
How can you treat these children in different ways?
    Since yesterday I've been tending the fire all night,
The whole night through, till the sky was all bright.
But you didn't get anything nice for me to eat;
All you got me was a bone that I could swallow.
    If I had been an unrelated beggar boy,
You still would have treated me to a jug of wine.
Now I am your own daughter, and yet you have

Banished me to the kitchen where I'm tending the fire.
The guests in the hall are all treated to dinner,
But your own daughter is shoved off to the kitchen.
Now place your hand on your heart and ponder
Whether you are fair and equitable or not at all!"
These words filled her mother with such rage
That she grabbed the poker and hit her daughter with it,
Most mercilessly, despite the feigned attempt
Of her brother's wife to come to her rescue.
Third Sister, beaten like this, was awash in tears.
"My dear mother, how considerate you truly are!
Which poor man will stay poor all through his life?
Since when have wealth and status grown roots?
Where are the green mountains without fruit trees?
Where in the world are there no poor people at all?
But as soon as our lives take a turn for the better,
I will come and inform you of the fact, my mother!"
When woman Wang heard this, she laughed heartily,
"Your boasting like a beggar is really ridiculous!
If your life indeed ever takes a turn for the better,
I will turn and twist in a foot-washing basin.
You beggar, I never want you to come back again,
Never again set foot inside the gate of this house!"
Upon these words, Third Sister cried hot tears;
With her son on her back she left to go back, and
As soon as she had stepped out the front gate,
Her mother closed and locked the gate behind her.

With every step she moved forward, she wept;
Tears coursed down her cheeks in great profusion.
Moving forward on her three-inch golden lotuses,
Tortured by hunger pangs—the road was a hard one.
As Third Sister was walking alongside the hills,
Her little boy on her back wept most piteously.
"My baby boy, you, too, feel the pangs of hunger
And want to drink some of your mother's milk."
Tears coursed down Third Sister's wet cheeks.

"Dear darling apple of my eye," she cried. "Alas,
Because your mother is beset by pangs of hunger,
She doesn't have any milk left for you to drink."

Third Sister placed her boy on a stone platform,
And she thereupon walked all along the hillside,
Looking for something she could give him to eat:
"My little boy is so hungry, so let's go back home."

Continuing along her road, she soon was home;
All of a sudden she arrived in front of her house.

As soon as her husband saw her, he addressed her,
"My dear wife," he called out again and again,
"When you went home yesterday you were so happy,
So why do you say not a word on your return?"

Third Sister answered her husband as follows:
"My dear husband, let me tell you what happened!

Eldest Sister was wearing clothes of gauze and silk;
Second Sister was wearing gold and silver jewelry.
But I was wearing these unpadded clothes, so
My mother had to curse me as soon as she saw me.

She earlier had urged me to marry someone else,
But I refused to marry a wealthy man with money.
When I returned home this time, I was still this poor,
So she shoved me off to the kitchen to tend the fire.

I tended the kitchen fire for her all through the night;
Because of that I was covered with sweat all over.
But she didn't give me anything good to eat at all;
All she got me was one bone that I could swallow!

She got Eldest Sister's little boy a leg of chicken,
She got Second Sister's little boy exactly the same,
But when our little boy felt the pangs of hunger,
All she gave him was just one old radish.

Our little boy is still young and doesn't understand,
So he grabbed the radish and swallowed it whole.
His grandmother then slapped him on the mouth;
She said he acted this way because he was a beggar!

When I saw my mother speaking in this way,
I told my mother that she was not fair and equitable:

Palm and backside of the hand are your own flesh,
So how can you treat your grandsons so differently?
    My mother could not stand me talking this way;
She grabbed the poker and started to beat me,
Without listening to any reason—this all despite
The feigned pleading for me by my elder sisters.
    It still would be a minor matter to get a beating,
But she also then chased me out of the house."
    When the husband had heard his wife's story,
He could not help but feel pain in his heart.
    "We, husband and wife, get along quite well;
We manage to survive by working hard in the fields.
But the people of this world are all so shallow;
They value only your clothes, not your character!
    When the husband has money, his wife is noble,
But people despise you when you have no money.
From now on we should be firmly determined
To give it our all to become the king of the hill!
    When man and wife do their plowing and spinning,
High Heaven has never betrayed their hard work.
Even the Yellow River at times is pure and clear,
So there must be a day when our fortune will turn.
    And if ever our fortune turns and we strike it rich,
A feud will requite a feud, a favor repay a favor!"

Let's not talk about the couple's industry and thrift
Yet another baby in her belly was about to be born.
    She stepped with her left foot in the embroidery room
While her right foot was still in the hall of the house:
Straddling the lintel of the door, she gave birth to a boy,
And husband and wife were both filled with joy.
    Water was poured in a foot-basin to wash his body;
Wrapped in a gauze skirt, he was given to his mother.
On the third day they selected a name for the baby;
The name they selected for him was Qimen.[8]
    "Your mother will raise you with greatest care, hoping
That life later will take a better turn for both of us."

This was the moment when her fortune turned:
Both her little boys lived to grow up into men.

Third Sister then addressed her husband as follows:
"My dear husband, please do not give in to sorrow!
A man who works hard will not have to worry about food;
A woman who works hard will wear something new.

    Freezing cold will not confront a woman who spins;
Hunger and famine will not starve a man who plows.
Ancient teachers of former times have said it well:
'It is only the hoe that doesn't reduce one to poverty.'"

    When the husband heard these words from his wife,
He got a hoe with a weight of three times five pounds.

    Up the hills he hoed the fields, up to the highest peak;
Down the hills he hoed the fields, down to the wetlands.
In the Sixth Month he still was hoeing the wetlands;
In the Tenth Month he cleared wasteland without mercy.

    He planted his fields with sorghum and also with wheat;
He planted them with corn and also with peanuts;
He planted them with radishes and also with buckwheat;
He also planted them with sweet potatoes for snacks.

All this industry and thrift of Third Sister and her man
Attracted the attention of the astral lord of Great White.[9]
He observed the hardships of both husband and wife,
The hardships they suffered and also their poverty.

    "The two sons who have been born to this couple
Actually are Stars of Literature from up in heaven.
If I were to wait another three years to help you out,
That would do in Third Sister and Xiao Hanting!"

    The metal star of Great White wasted no time:
"I will gift that couple of mine with both gold and silver!"[10]

As soon as Hanting saw that the sky was bright,
He took his hoe and went up into the mountain woods.
From early morning till noontime he kept on digging,
And from noontime till dusk he kept on digging.

Eventually he reached a black slab of stone, and
Below that slab of stone he found gold and silver.
At the sight of that treasure he was filled with joy,
And he carried it back home with the greatest haste.

At the sight of all this gold and silver Third Sister
Thanked Heaven and Earth and also all the gods:
"Today High Heaven shows us His protection by
Gifting us, husband and wife, with this gold and silver."

When they then had taken a close look at the silver,
They saw that each and every bar carried the legend "Qimen."

Husband and wife did not waste any time but
Thanked the gods with incense and paper money.
They bought a pig and a goat and fine wine and
Offered these in sacrifice to the god of the soil.

When husband and wife had returned to the house,
The gold and silver were stored in the embroidery room.
Each of the next three years were greatly profitable,
And people now counted them among the wealthy.

They grew sticky grain to make their own wine,
Alcohol from glutinous grain to entertain their guests.
The constant stream of visitors coming to their house
Claimed to be either relatives or good friends.

They bought five hundred *mu* of fields wet and dry;
The entrance gate and the rooms were all made new.
With plenty of clothes to wear and rice to eat, they
Remembered those days when they had to borrow.

"When others borrowed from us: a stream in the hills;
When we borrowed from others: frost in midsummer!
Today, now our fortune has turned, we as a couple
Thank Heaven and Earth and all the numinous gods!"

Sanyuan at that time was just fifteen years of age,
And Qimen had reached the age of thirteen.

The two brothers studied their letters in school and
Submitted their essays and were admitted as students.
After three years of study, knowing rites and meaning,

They had read all the books from beginning to end.
They heard that the court was holding its great examination,
Summoning all cultured people from the whole world.
The two brothers did not waste a moment but
Packed their luggage and promptly set out on the road.

Upon arriving in the provincial capital and finding an inn,
The brothers came to the gate of the examination grounds.
Their three examination essays were done very well,
And the examination official read them attentively.

When some days later the list of dragons was posted,
They looked at it to see who had passed the exam:
The very first name on the list was Xiao Sanyuan,
And the number two on the list was Xiao Qimen!

Seeing their listing, the brothers were filled with joy,
A joy that showed on their faces, a smile in their hearts!
They hurried to pack their luggage and travel home,
Where close and distant relatives welcomed them.

Loudly resounding—the music of pipes and drums:
Two brothers had passed the examination together!
"Elder and younger brother both equally successful."
This inscription was hung above the gate to the hall!

Let's not talk of the riches and glory of the Xiao family;
Let's talk again about the situation of the Wang family.
In earlier days woman Wang had been immensely rich,
But now her fortunes lagged compared to those of others.

Preferring riches to poverty, they allowed other people to die;
With false balances and bushels they cheated the poor.
The Jade Emperor thereupon sent down an edict
Ordering disasters to descend to the world of dust.

The disaster of fire struck the house of Eldest Sister;
The disaster of fire struck the house of Second Sister;
The disaster of fire struck the house of the Wang family:
Three astral lords had descended to the world of dust!

The house of Eldest Sister was hit by Heaven's fire,
And in three years' time no fewer than nine people died.
The house of Second Sister was visited by misfortune,

And in a single year three people lost their lives, and so
In three years' time no fewer than nine people died.
    The house of woman Wang met with dismal disasters,
And all fields and farms, houses and barns were sold.
Once all the people had died and the money was spent,
The only one left was woman Wang, all alone.
    In her house she did not have rice for tomorrow,
And she didn't have any good clothes to wear anymore.
The elderly woman Wang had no one to care for her,
And she survived by begging for rice in the streets.
    During daytime she begged for rice at a thousand places;
At night she slept in old temples and open pavilions.
When people in the streets listened to her tale of woe,
Each and every one told her she was an evil woman.

She had walked to many houses to beg for some rice,
And, [bitten by] dogs, she was all covered with blood.
She was freezing all over and feeling the pangs of hunger,
And she hadn't gone out of the house for three days on end.
    Her head was dizzy from hunger, her eyes were blurred;
Freezing and starving, she was shivering all over her body.
She had no other option but to go out into the streets, and
By accident arrived in front of Third Sister's house.
    Woman Wang called out loudly in front of the gate,
Calling, "Milady!" and "Young ladies!" again and again.
"I here am an elderly person with no one to care for her;
Alas, if I think of it, I am without husband or children.
    If you have rice in the house, please give me a mouthful,
And you will save this old woman from imminent death.
I depend on donations from others, and their virtuous deeds,
A virtue bringing wealth and status to sons and daughters."
    When Third Sister heard this voice outside the gate,
She opened the door of her room to listen more closely.
And when she left her room to have a better look,
It turned out after all that it was her own mother!
    When woman Wang lifted her head to have a look,
She realized that this great lady was her third daughter.

Woman Wang immediately addressed her as follows:
"My dear darling apple of my eye," she cried out.

"Your mother, my darling child, now has grown old,
Please be so kind as to save me from imminent death.
Today mother and daughter have been reunited again:
Flowers bloom once again, the moon is full again!"

These words of her mother angered our Third Sister:
"My dear mother, now please listen to me for a while.
I thought that you would be rich and mighty forever.
Who could have guessed that today you'd be poor?

Isn't my eldest sister your own daughter, and hasn't
My second sister always been the apple of your eye?
Let my two elder sisters come and take care of you—
The rich and mighty take care of the rich and mighty.

But today you have come to this house of beggars—
How can we take care of someone made of gold and jade?
We poor starving beggars haven't got any rice to eat,
So how could we spare some rice to feed someone else?"

Tears coursed down the cheeks of old woman Wang.
"My dear daughter, please listen to what I have to say.
You hate me because of your earlier bitter sufferings,
But like cold water rinsing rice, don't remember them!"

When Third Sister heard these words from her mother,
She could not help but feel an inkling of daughterly love.
"Of course I should keep her here and take care of her,
But her behavior in those days was really too inhuman!

If I refuse to keep her here and take care of her,
It's bound to be the death of this woman without support.
It is far better that she should have been in the wrong,
But that should not distort my feelings as her child.

It may be a minor matter not to take care of my mother,
But I would acquire a worldwide reputation as unfilial.
Today I'll make sure that she doesn't flaunt her nature,
To prevent her from acting again as she did before."

So, feigning rage, she cursed her mother,

"Disappear as fast as you can and go to those others!
My eldest sister and second sister are rich and mighty;
They will feed you with delicate fare and fine food.

We here at home eat only porridge made from corn;
Sweet potatoes and peanuts are the snacks we have.
I'm afraid that such poor fare doesn't suite your palate;
Remember never again to come and beg at my door."

Third Sister opened the two wings of the gate and
Walked straight inside, into the hall of the house.

When woman Wang saw that her daughter was gone,
Tears coursed down her cheeks in great profusion.

"In the past it was me, your mother, who wronged you;
Now today you do not recognize the bonds of blood.
But if today my own daughter will not recognize me,
I will starve myself to death here in front of her gate."

Just as old woman Wang was crying her heart out,
Both her two grandsons were coming back home.

As they walked up to the gate, they asked her, saying:
"Beggar woman, please tell us, what is your name?
For what reason have you now come to our place?
You are crying so much that tears flow down your cheeks."

Woman Wang immediately spoke the following words:
"My dear young masters, please listen to what I say.
I hail from Yongzhou Prefecture in Hunan,
To the east of the prefectural capital—I'm called Wang.

Old woman Wang who begs for rice—that is me.
And your mother Third Sister, she is my daughter.
Today I came here to your house, begging for rice,
Because I couldn't stand the hunger in my stomach.

For three days on end I haven't had any food at all;
My head is dizzy from hunger and my eyes are blurred.
Dear young masters, please show some compassion
And please give me something to eat, anything!"

Her two grandsons then spoke the following words:
"Grandmother, please listen to what we have to say.

There is no need for you to continue to shed tears;
It just so happens we had been out on business."

When the two brothers entered the embroidery room,
 [They said,] "Dear mother, please listen to our words.
    When that beggar woman came here begging for rice,
Shouldn't you have invited her inside the house?
Please explain your intentions to us in great detail
As we do not understand why you acted this way."
    Third Sister immediately answered them as follows:
"My sons, there are certain matters you don't know.
That year, when your grandmother turned fifty-one,
I went there with Sanyuan to offer congratulations.
    At home we were dirt-poor and couldn't manage,
So I had no birthday candles and boxes of presents.
Your grandmother felt nothing but contempt for you.
We, mother and son, were shoved off to the kitchen.
    The second day, when a banquet was spread at noon
To the loudly resounding music of pipes and drums,
All the guests in the hall sat down to dinner there,
But the two of us, mother and son, we were excluded!
    She gave Eldest Sister's little boy a leg of chicken,
She gave Second Sister's little boy a leg of chicken,
But alas, when my little baby also was hungry,
She gave him a radish—he swallowed it whole.
    Your grandmother the millionaire beat you twice
And cursed you, saying you were born to be a beggar.
When I saw that, I really could not stand it at all;
I told my mother she was not fair and equitable.
    'Palm and backside of the hand are your own flesh,
So how can you treat your grandsons so differently?'
Your grandmother couldn't stand me talking this way,
And so she grabbed a poker to give me a beating.
    It would have been a minor matter to be beaten,
But she also then and there chased me out of the house.
In full sight of all the guests filling the high hall,

She did not show any feeling of motherly love!
    This was all the fault of my mother, her doing!
Rich and mighty she didn't recognize anyone poor.
Now she herself has fallen on hard times, so today
She comes here and claims we are flesh and blood.
    In those days she felt only contempt for us all;
She didn't know love between mother and daughter.
My sons, don't keep trying to change my mind;
Let her starve to death right in front of our gate!"

When the children heard their mother's argument,
They knelt down on their knees before their mother.
The two brothers urged her to change her mind.
"Dear mother, please listen to what we have to say.
    Your mother suffered, carrying you for ten months;
As human beings we must repay our parents' grace.
If one doesn't take care of one's parents while they're alive,
One has lived in vain in the eyes of High Heaven.
    In this world it is loyalty and filial piety that count:
A minister repays his lord's grace, a child his parents'.
Raising a son who doesn't repay his mother's hardship,
One raises a daughter who'll repay her parents' favors.
    If you don't believe us, look at the water from the roof:
Each and every drop drips down in the very same spot!
The ancient teachers of bygone days said it well:
'One never should say one's mother is lacking in love.'
    We, your children, are kneeling down before you,
Hoping that you, our mother, will show some heart.
As long as you don't ask grandmother to come inside,
We will go on kneeling in front of you and not get up.
    Our grandmother may have behaved improperly,
But she is closest kin related to us by flesh and blood!"
    When Third Sister heard these words from her sons,
Joy appeared on her face, a smile in her heart.
"People who are filial have children who are filial;
Those who are unfilial will have unfilial offspring."

She promptly addressed her two sons as follows:
"My two dear darling sons, please rise to your feet.
You go and invite your grandmother to come inside;
Your mother never had any other intention at all."

Hearing this, the two brothers were filled with joy,
And they invited their grandmother to come inside.
    They led her to the high hall, asked her to take a seat,
And they then poured her a cup of most fragrant tea.
Their grandmother addressed them in these words:
"My dear gentlemen, please tell me who you are."
    Sanyuan immediately answered her as follows:
"We are your own grandsons of a different surname."
    Hearing this, their grandmother was filled with joy:
"Then you must be Qimen, my youngest grandchild!
I've heard that you passed the court examinations,
And that you two brothers have achieved great fame!"
    Sanyuan stayed with his grandmother in the high hall,
While Qimen went to the kitchen to heat up the fire.
When he had heated a bowl of clean and pure water,
He took the foot-washing basin to the embroidery room.
    The grandmother washed herself in the embroidery room,
And Third Sister opened her chests to take out clothes.
She selected a shirt and a skirt made of silk and satin
And gave these to her mother to wear from now on.
    The old lady once again was properly dressed,
And to top it off, she wore a skirt made of gauze.
They invited her to come and sit in the high hall:
The whole family, old and young, one happy smile!
    Mother and daughter spoke frankly to each other;
Then the old lady returned to the embroidery room.
She was treated to the finest foods and delicacies,
Spending her days in luxury, glory, status, and wealth.

She was filially provided with three meals each day;
The clothes she wore were made of silk and wool.

When she got up each morning, she had washing water,
And at night a dry blanket provided her comfort.
  Her luxury, glory, status, and wealth cannot be told,
But woman Wang was not made out for such blessings.
One or two years after she arrived at the Xiaos,
Her legs started to swell up, and her stomach was struck.
  This was all because her sins had been so many;
She could not walk with ease, not even sit with ease.
Once woman Wang had fallen ill in their house,
The whole family, old and young, were concerned.
  They hurriedly invited a doctor to come, but alas,
The medicines that were prescribed didn't work.
The best recipe cannot cure a case caused by karma:
The exorcist commanded his ghosts all to no avail!
  Woman Wang passed away to return to the shades;
The whole family, old and young, wept piteously.
  They invited monks to open the way [for the coffin];
The monks opened the way and recited their sutras.
Close and distant relatives came to mourn the deceased,
Noisily reciting the sutras and bowing to the Buddha.
  The ceremonies of the seven Sevens were completed,
And to the loudly resounding music of pipes and drums,
She was buried by the main road outside the east gate.
The geomantic location was chosen by a specialist.
  Cypress and pine were planted in front of the grave.
At each of the four seasons she received offerings,
And when travelers passing by saw all this going on,
All said that Third Sister manifested a filial heart.

Let's not talk about woman Wang and her death;
Let's tell again about Third Sister and her situation.
  Since ancient times good people have suffered many hardships,
And they establish themselves after many tribulations.
If one has not suffered the greatest hardship of them all,
One cannot end up as the best, above all others.
  Third Sister was a woman who practiced filial piety;

Those who are filial will have children who are filial.
Later both her two sons entered the bureaucracy,
And the whole family enjoyed the imperial grace.

Let me urge all true gentlemen of the whole world,
All men and women, to remember this in their hearts:
If each and every one will stick to this book's message,
Sons and grandsons will later never suffer poverty.
     You gentlemen of leisure who are reading books,
May the earlier generation teach this to the later.
Now I've told this ballad in verse to its conclusion:
May she remain famous forever, for all eternity!

6

THE DAUGHTER OF THE XIAO FAMILY

Written out by Gao Yinxian

From the moment Pangu divided heaven and earth,
Each and every emperor has had his own ministers.
Light and shadow, arrowlike, urge one on to old age;
Sun and moon resemble a shuttle and never once stop.

Flowers bloom only to fall: your beauty easily fades;
Yesterday's people suddenly disappear from sight.
I'll not sing of an earlier dynasty or of the Later Han;[1]
I will sing the tale of a person from Nanhui County.

Sir Liu of Nanhui County was exceedingly rich;
He came from a very rich family and was married.
He had been married to his wife for more than ten years,
And still the couple had no son, and lacked a daughter.

Husband and wife together reached a decision:
They would make donations for the sake of the poor.
Behind their estate was the Stone Dragon Monastery;
It had lain in ruins for no one knew how many years.

They first repaired the towers and the Buddha-hall;
They next restored the images and the Guanyin statue.
They also promised five hundred pairs of silk sandals;

Five hundred *kasayas* hung from the temple gate.[2]
  After a full month the towers had been restored;
Forty-nine days were spent in thanking the gods.
At that time lady Ma once experienced a dream;
In that dream she saw a red sun atop her body.

    Those who dream of a red sun give birth to a boy;
Those who dream of a bright moon give birth to a girl.
On top of that she also dreamt of a string of red silk:
Left and right on her hands—a repeated vision.

    From the moment lady Ma saw this dream,
She was indeed since that dream heavy with child.
Other people carry a baby for a full ten months,
But lady Ma carried her baby for one full year.

    After exactly one year her term was up,
And she gave birth to a baby boy, with great pain.
Water was poured in a golden bowl to bathe the baby,
And they chose for him the name Liu Wenliang.

    They invited a diviner to compute his fate,
And they told him in detail all the circumstances:
He was born in a *dingmao* year, a *guiyou* month;
He was born on a *yimao* day, on a *jimao* hour.

    To compute this fate was not a mean matter, as
Later he would study books, reach high office.

At the ages of one and two he was very quick-witted;
At the ages of three and four he grew into manhood.
Very soon he had grown to the age of six or seven;
Once sent to school, he proved himself very intelligent.

    First he wrote "up," "time," fish," "hill," "stream";
Later he read the Odes and the Documents, all the Classics.
He fully understood the Five Works and the Four Books,
And he memorized the school's Book of Changes.[3]

    Right at that time the court announced an examination,
And Wenliang wanted to participate in order to achieve fame.
As soon as sir Liu heard him talk of this intention,
He discussed the situation with his wife lady Ma.

"Our son's real concern is not about achieving fame;
The reason is that we have not yet found him a wife."
Once husband and wife had reached this conclusion,
They invited matchmakers from all over the place.

One invited matchmaker was one Zhang Xuwu,
Who gave them a full and circumstantial account:
"The Xiao family of West Lake has a daughter
Who has just turned fifteen—a most fitting match!

Rouge and powder, green leaves, [eyes like] pools,
Cheeks like peach petals, with an inkling of spring:
I've seen the fairest flowers of one hundred towns,
But she resembles a seated Guanyin with her vase!"[4]

Having heard these words, sir Liu was filled with joy,
And he immediately dispatched the matchmaker.

He invited a diviner to compute the couple's future fate—
"The male side belongs to Earth, the female to Fire;
These generating each other, father and son are at peace.
For all of their lives they will never be separated;
The withered flower on the rock is not transplanted."

Sir Liu had heard about this daughter of the Xiaos.
"Heaven allowed you to meet this matchmaker!"

First he sent a chicken and a goose and engagement gifts;
Then he sent a pig and a goat and the wedding gold.
They selected the year and month and a lucky day;
Flowers are red, leaves green: the bride entered the gate.

Wenliang and lady Xiao met each other face to face;
They venerated the ancestors, honored his parents,
And when Wenliang had drunk the cup of union,
These two mandarin ducks became a fine couple.

Not long after the marriage, after only three days,
On the fourth day he wanted to leave to seek fame.
First he went to the hall to say good-bye to his parents;
Then he went to his room to say good-bye to his wife.

Lady Xiao then spoke to her husband as follows:
"Now please listen carefully to what I have to say.

If this is because you dislike me for being so ugly—
Marriage bonds are determined by our former lives.
If this is because you think my dowry was too small,
I'll go back home and inform my father and mother."
　　Wenliang answered his wife in the following way:
"My dear wife, all this has nothing to do with you!
[I would not dare suggest that you might be ugly;]
I wouldn't dare complain your dowry was too small.

　　When a man turns fifteen and still holds no office,
He resembles a precious mirror that doesn't shine.
When a girl turns fifteen without needle and thread,
She sits idly in her room, only [wasting] her mind.

　　You will take care of my dear mother in the hall;
I rely on you, my dear wife, to serve them well.
Provide them with their daily meals, tea, and wine;
Make sure the courtyard there is in proper order!"

　　Lady Xiao promptly answered her husband thus:
"My dear husband, please listen to what I will say.

　　Of course I'll respectfully serve my parents-in-law;
There's no need for you to explain my duties to me.
But if you, my husband, truly want to seek fame,
What kind of mementos will you leave with me?"

　　"I leave you your parents-in-law as a memento,
I leave our fields and farms for you to manage,
And then I leave the red sun as a third memento:
These three mementos all will never change!"

　　Lady Xiao answered him in the following way:
"These three mementos all are bound to change.
[You leave me my parents-in-law as a memento:]
My elderly parents-in-law—how many more years?

　　You leave me the fields and farms as a memento,
But I fear it may be hard to bring in the harvest.
And then you leave me the red sun as a memento—
But each day, I fear, it is bound to sink in the west!

　　I, too, have three things that may serve as mementos;
I will give them to you, and then you may leave.
This pair of silken sandals may serve as a memento—

Each and every stitch was done with utmost care.
This one golden hairpin may serve as a memento—
Wrought by the silversmith, it is not to be despised.
And this bronze mirror may serve as a memento.
I will give these to you, and then you may leave."

When Wenliang had received these three mementos,
He put them in his book box and promptly took off.
"Husband and wife from now on will be separated—
Do not blindly go without a companion on the road.

As the sun appears in the east, in the bright sky:
May you quickly return from your search for office!
I will respectfully serve both your parents in the hall;
No need for you to worry about them day and night!

As the sun appears in the east, in the bright sky:
Return home when you have achieved high office!
As the sun appears in the east, in the bright sky—
Don't you worry at all once you have left!

From now on I will be a peach tree or a plum tree
That never meets the month of spring, never blooms.
Do not pluck the wildflowers you'll find by the road;
Do not blindly go without a companion on the road."

Wenliang then answered his wife in the following way:
"Please, now do go back and return to the house!
There never will be any end to this back and forth!
What's the need to explain his duties to your husband?"

Lady Xiao then wanted to offer him one cup of wine.
"Then you immediately mount your horse and take off!"
She took the golden-thread wine jug and raised it high,
While folding chairs were set out opposite each other.

To the left they hung a picture of Zhang Guolao;
To the right they hung a picture of Lü Dongbin.[5]
She then ordered her servant girl to pour the wine.
"I offer you four cups of wine to ease my mind.

With the first cup of wine I wish you a safe journey;
With the fourth cup I wish you will keep my heart."[6]

When Wenliang had finished the four cups of wine,
He immediately mounted his horse and departed.

His mind occupied only by the search for fame,
He never turned his head back to look at his wife.

When lady Xiao saw that her husband had left,
She could not help being flooded by tears.
   "That little clump of willow trees there by the river
Hinders me from following my husband with my eyes.
If only I had an ax in my hands, I would
Uproot them all, so I could watch him as he goes!"
   Lady Xiao turned around and returned to her house;
In one straight line she walked back to the house.
The first watch and second watch, she sat in her room;
The third watch and fourth watch, in chilly darkness.
   She sat there till the fifth watch, in darkest silence,
When a couple of geese honked a number of times.
"They must have lost their companion at nighttime,
So they are in the same situation as people like me."

Let's drop the subject of lady Xiao, not sing of her,
But let's sing again of Wenliang and his situation.
After thirty-five miles it was peach blossom trees;
After forty-five miles it was apricot blossom village.
   The song cannot tell of each stage of his journey,
And soon be beheld the walls of the city of Beijing.
Inside the city of Beijing a placard had been posted:
All kinds of people were being sought and selected.
   At this sight Wenliang's heart was filled with joy;
Fully prepared he lodged in the imperial buildings.
When he had composed three excellent essays,
He was the only person left of all the exam candidates.
   As soon as he had handed them in to Wang Wangji,[7]
The latter personally ranked him as the top of the list.
   His first appointment was to be prefect of Kainan;
His second appointment was to be a big shot in Hunan;
His third appointment was to be an inspector in Nanjing:
All in a hurry suddenly eighteen years had passed!

Let's not sing anymore at all about that Wenliang;
Let's sing again about lady Xiao, that kind of person.
With a husband a thousand days pass in a flash, but
Without a husband even a single day is hard to bear.

From early dawn she watched for her husband till noon;
From dusk she watched for him till daybreak.

"When he left, he said he'd come back after three years,
But for eighteen years we haven't received any news.
Right now, I find, it is the thirtieth, New Year's Eve,
And we still have not received any news from him!"

When she saw that New Year's Day, the first, had arrived,
And all other families were celebrating the new year,
Lady Xiao put on her finery and also dressed up,
And moving lightly with tiny steps, she left her room.

She asked her parents-in-law to be seated in the hall;
She bowed down on her knees in the dust of the floor.[8]
Her mother-in-law raised her up with both her hands,
Repeatedly crying out, "My dear child, my dear child!

Since your husband left, eighteen years have passed,
And here at home we never, never received any news.
To his shame he has cut all ties with his two parents,
So you now would do better to marry someone else!"

When lady Xiao heard them talking in this manner,
She could not help being flooded with tears.

"If it is indeed the case that my husband has died,
I will wear the white of mourning, follow the rites.
I'll not apply rouge or powder, not wear any flowers,
Not apply any cosmetics—so I will live out my days."

"Mourning for a husband is completed in three years—
Allow your parents-in-law to explain the situation.
We have to fear that our son is not alive anymore,
So why don't you marry someone else and have a life?

Look at one of our neighbors, young master Song:
He is a fine young fellow and extremely reliable.
Let's ask him to come to our house as a son-in-law,
So he can take care of us two for the rest of our lives."

Lady Xiao promptly answered her parents-in-law.
"My dear parents-in-law, please listen to my words.

A good horse will not carry two different saddles;
A good woman will not be married to two husbands.
No one can ride a horse that is carrying two saddles;
A woman with two husbands has a bad reputation.

If you want to force me to marry someone else,
I will absolutely refuse to marry a second husband!
The first vow I swear here is as big as heaven:
Only if carps climb up bamboo will I marry again.

The second vow I swear here is as big as heaven:
Only if the Yellow River runs dry will I marry again.
The third vow I swear here is as big as heaven:
Only if a horse grows horns will I marry again!"

Her parents-in-law heard lady Xiao and knew
That these three vows set impossible conditions.
In all the biggest and longest rivers for all eternity—
No one ever saw carps climb up bamboo poles.

Even during a nine-year famine, a terrible drought,
No one ever saw the Yellow River run dry.
The king of Qi collected a million horses, but
No one saw any of these horses grow horns.[9]

Lady Xiao refused to marry a second husband,
And each day she wept and was awash in tears.

This disturbed the astral lord of Great White,[10]
And he promptly descended to earth to ask her,
"Filial woman, why do you weep day in, day out?
What is the problem that so wounds your heart?"

Lady Xiao answered as follows: "Dear granddad!
Dear granddad, please listen to what I have to say.
I am a daughter of the Xiao family of West Lake, and
When I was married, my husband was Liu Wenliang.

Three days with my man inside red-gauze bed curtains—
And on the fourth day he wanted to leave and search for fame.
At the time he said he'd come back after three years,

But even after eighteen years we have had no letter.
　　My parents-in-law now urge me to marry again, but
I do not want ever to marry a second husband at all.
Because I don't know what to do either way,
I see no way out but to jump into this river and die."
　　The graybeard promptly answered her as follows:
"My dear woman, please stop crying! Your husband
Has achieved high office and is very much alive.
Currently he is still occupied as an inspector in Beijing.
　　Right now this student enjoys the emperor's favor.
On your behalf I will send your husband a dream—
I'm a manifestation of Great White. Lady, good-bye!
Your husband this very day will start out for home."

When lady Xiao heard the words of the graybeard,
She immediately turned around and went back home.
The astral lord of Great White transformed himself
And immediately dispatched a dream to her husband.
　　When Wenliang had fallen asleep, he had a dream, and
In his dream he saw a single bird soaring into the clouds.
He also dreamt of the wide expanse of the Yellow River
And thousands of boats crossing the sea—such a dream.
　　Startled awake, Wenliang fell to thinking and said,
"Go and find me a specialist to interpret my dreams!"
The Star of Metal of Great White transformed himself;
He presented himself to Wenliang to explain his dream.
　　The latter narrated his dreams in detail to Great White.
"Astral lord, please allow me to tell you the situation;
From the very beginning I will tell you all the details.
　　In my dream I saw a single bird soaring into the clouds."
"Your wife does not want to marry a second husband."
"I also dreamt of the wide expanse of the Yellow River!"
"After all these years you still long for your parents."
"I also dreamt of thousands of ships crossing the ocean."
"Tomorrow morning at dawn you'll start out for home."
　　When Wenliang heard him provide this explanation,

He promptly wrote a request to submit to the emperor.
When his king had received it, he gave his permission:
"Return home tomorrow in order to serve your parents!"
    When the emperor saw that he acted out of filial piety,
That he wanted to return out of longing for his parents,
[He awarded him a plaque] reading "Revering the rites,
He serves his parents" to be displayed above the gate.

Guarding against leaving only for pine tree and cypress,[11]
He took his leave of his lord and promptly set out.
In one day he covered a stretch of three hundred miles;
His horse ran as fast as the wind, as if carried by clouds.
    After only a single day he came to the county of Nanhui,
Where every family welcomed this important official.
But when he arrived at the pond in front of the mine,
He noticed there a woman all awash in tears.
    With bamboo pins in her hair she was in mourning,
Fully clad in white clothes, she [was free of] attachments.
Our civil official stepped forward and asked this woman:
"To which family do you belong? Where are you from?"
    The woman promptly answered the official as follows:[12]
"Please listen carefully to me as I tell you my story.
    I am a woman from West Lake here in this county, and
When I was married, my husband was surnamed Liu.
When I had lived with him for three days as a couple,
He wanted to leave on the fourth day in order to achieve fame.
    At that time he said he would be back after three years,
But by now he has been gone for a full eighteen years.
I do not know whether my husband is still alive or not,
As news from him has never reached our house.
    My parents-in-law are urging me to marry once again,
But I definitely do not want to marry someone else.
If they really bring someone into the house for me,
I see no way out but jumping into this river to die!"
    When the official had heard the woman's tale,
He knelt down to the side [and said,] "Please listen—
Your husband Wenliang has not died, he's alive!

He serves at court as an official, is quite renowned!

He and I were born in the same year, the same month;
We received our lives on the same day, the same hour.
He departed from the imperial capital together with me;
He is bound to arrive in this place tomorrow."

"If indeed my husband returns home on that day,
With lowered head I'll thank you for your good grace."

After receiving her four bows, the official left.
When she returned home, she told her parents-in-law,
"Yesterday an official passed through this place
Who was exactly like my husband in all respects!"

Before she was done speaking, that official arrived.
All day long people were busily making preparations.
Sir Liu explained this to the official as follows:
"Ever since our son left, he has taken his ease,

But here at home that leaves us with a problem.
So now we'll marry off his wife to someone else.
I have decided that today he will join the family—
At midnight the marriage will be consummated!"

When the official heard this tale from him,
He stubbornly refused to leave the hall of the house,
As he wanted to see who was coming to take his place,
And which woman would dare act as the matchmaker.

The official promptly replied, "My dear lady Xiao,
The day will come when Wenliang returns home.
If indeed Wenliang is bound to return this very day,
There will be a son who will not greet his parents!"

Sir Liu promptly spoke to the official as follows:
"For a full eighteen years we have had no news!
My son for a fact definitely must have passed on,
So now we will marry his wife to someone else."

The official loudly cursed. . . .
Kneeling before the hall, he bowed to his parents,[13]
"I am your own son; I am the seed of your loins.
My full name is nothing else but Liu Wenliang!

Since I said good-bye to my parents and departed,

Indeed no news or letter ever arrived at this house.
Through my excess of loyalty I failed in filial piety,
But now I've returned home to serve my parents."

When lady Xiao heard him give this account,
She came running from her room to find out the truth.
"If you indeed are my husband who has come home,
Then show me the mementos that will serve as proof."
    First he got the silk sandals that were a memento,
Then he got the gold hairpin that served as a memento,
Third he got the bronze mirror that was a memento:
When he got those mementos, she was filled with joy.
    She dressed herself in the phoenix cap and gown;
Together they entered the hall and bowed to his parents.

After his return, Wenliang fathered two sons,
And later these two brothers also both achieved fame:
The eldest son achieved the rank of third on the list;[14]
The youngest son achieved the rank of top of the list.

7

LADY LUO

Written out by Yi Nianhua

Since the time when Pangu opened up heaven and earth,[1]
How many emperors and long-lived lords have there been?
How many people were blessed and ascended the golden steps?[2]
How many were unfortunate and died in the border regions?
　　How many people rest at night behind red gauze curtains?
How many people are without a blanket till break of dawn?
How many people have plenty of rice—but nobody eats it?
How many people have no rice at all and boil clear water?
　　How many people have no wife at all and live all alone?
How many people have three women to serve one husband?
How many people in this world live to the age of one hundred?
And how many people die all of a sudden in their rooms?

Tripitaka of the Tang fetched sutras from the Western Paradise,[3]
Whereas Mulian went to the underworld to find his mother.[4]
Self-sacrifice from a sense of duty: the Jade Maiden's tale;[5]
Ding Lan carved a statue of wood in order to see his mother.[6]
　　By the lake she waited for her husband: the fate of lady Xiao;[7]
In the grave she joined her husband: the story of Zhu Yingtai.[8]

Trekking a thousand miles to deliver clothes: Meng Jiangnü—
That chaste-hearted young woman traveled to join her husband.⁹

I'll not tell all kind of tales about these married couples—
In all of these cases their fates were determined by their karma.
I could go on without end telling tales of filial obedience,
But what I will sing will be the tale of Qiuhu and lady Luo.
   Qiuhu's family had been immensely rich for generations:
No bird could fly from end to end across their fields and farms!
A matchmaker came to his house to tell of lady Luo, saying
They were a couple made in heaven, a truly perfect match.

   When he saw the engagement letter, his joy knew no bounds,
Because the two of them were exactly the same age in years.
He selected a fitting hour together with an appropriate day
And sent the wedding gifts over along with a pig and a goat.
   The matchmaker hurried over to the Luo family and said
That the wedding gifts from the Luos had arrived at the gate.
This was reported to the young lady Luo in her room,
And they told her to get dressed and to do up her hair.

   She combed her hair and tied it up in a coiling-dragon bun;
The golden pins she put in her hair gave off a brilliant dazzle.
When she walked, she did not move her feet below her skirt;
She looked just like Guanyin when she leaves her temple.¹⁰

   One person said she was a priceless treasure worth millions;
As people commented on her appearance, voices ran high!
Golden pins stuck in her hair and also one sprig of flowers,
The silk shoes on her feet were only three inches long.

   When she had fully dressed and finished her toilette,
She was an immortal maiden as she came out of her room.
"Now eighteen years ago I was born as your daughter,
But today I leave my mother's house, going off to marry."

   She took her leave of the ancestors and the burning incense;
She took her leave of her parents as she left the village.
"Eighteen years ago my father married my mother;
Now I am dressed in wedding dress and leave your house."

The first three days after her arrival: behind red gauze curtains!
The fourth day following her arrival her husband was an official.

"A letter has arrived from the court this very last night,
Inviting me to go down there to become a high official!"
    Lady Luo replied to her husband in the following manner:
"My dear husband, please listen to what I have to say.

    Is this perhaps because you hate me because I am so ugly,
Or is it perhaps because you think my dowry was too small?
If you think my dowry was too small, there's no problem,
Because in that case I'll go back home and tell my parents."

    "It is not because I would dare complain that you are ugly;
It is not because I dare think that your dowry is too small.
But if a man at the age of fifteen still has no appointment,
He in vain acts the part of a man—he should put in the effort!"

    "If a woman at the age of fifteen has no needle and thread,
She in vain acts a daughter's part in the room of her mother.

    I offer you one cup of wine to wish you a pleasant journey;
I offer you a second cup of wine so you'll keep my heart.
I offer you a third cup of wine as you mount your horse;
I offer you a fourth cup of wine—may you quickly return!

    If you manage to become an official, serve for three years;
If you fail to become an official, return within half a year.
Other people who see their husbands off give him a horse,
But now when I see my husband off, I give him all my love.

    Seeing you off, I see you off up to the knoll of green grass,
And I urge you, my dear husband, to be honest and true.
Don't wildly pluck the flowers you may find on the road,
As you have your own sprig of flowers back at home!"

Her husband became an official and served for nine years,
And not even a single letter ever arrived at his home!

Once when Qiuhu fell asleep, he had a dream in his sleep,
And in this dream he saw his own father and mother.
There were two bright lamps, but only one shone clearly;
There were two flowering trees, but only one was all red.

    He asked a diviner to come and interpret his dream;
The diviner interpreted his dream: it was unfavorable.
Once he knew that his parents would not last much longer,
He immediately yearned to go back to his parental home.

When he arrived at a bridge, he brought his horse to a stop, as
He encountered a woman plucking mulberry leaves.

"Who are you, pretty little girl, and tell me, why do
You go out all by yourself plucking mulberry leaves?
To which family do you belong, little slave girl, and why
Do you go out all by yourself plucking mulberry leaves?"

The girl answered His Excellency in the following words:
"Your Excellency, please listen to what I have to say.

I belong to the Luo family, I am a daughter of the Luos,
And the husband I was married to is called Luo Qiuhu.
My husband has been an official now for nine years,
But not even a single letter ever arrived at our house."

His Excellency answered the girl in the following words:
"Little girl, please listen to what I have to say to you!
Of every ten people who become officials, nine die;
The roads are strewn with their bones, as white as frost.

Why don't you get together with me as husband and wife,
Why don't we become a pair of fine mandarin ducks?
If you want gold and silver, I have plenty of both;
If you want linen and silks, I will open my boxes!"

"The last thing I want is your gold or your silver;
The last thing I'll touch is your silver or gold!"
When he heard the girl, he said not a word in reply
But mounted his horse, turned back, and went home.

When he arrived in his village and entered the room,
He greeted his parents, thanking them for their grace.
He invited his parents to take their seats in the high hall:
"Your young son has come home to serve the two of you."

Then he asked for lady Luo so he might greet her—
"Lady Luo is not in your mother's room at present.
She has raised many silkworms that all need to eat,
So she took off her silks to gather mulberry leaves."

Lady Luo made her toilette and dressed herself up,
Lightly moving with small steps, she came from her room.
When she had greeted her husband, she made a deep bow,
And after making her bow, she returned to her room.

"Earlier on you were the one who tried to seduce me;
You tried to seduce me to marry somebody else.
Whereas I, the woman, was a chaste-hearted woman,
You, the man, are a man without heart and guts!"

The story tells she had lived these nine years alone,
But a single night with Qiuhu was too much to bear!

She took her leave of the bed and cushion in her room.
"I will never again enjoy pleasure on this bed!"
She took her leave of the clothes racks in her room.
"I will never again take my clothes from these racks!"
  She took her leave of the pair of boxes in her room.
"I will never again take any clothes from these boxes!"
She took her leave of the single lamp in her room.
"As long as you have no oil, you will not shine!"
  She took her leave of the toilet-table in her room.
"Never again will I sit before you to make my toilette!"
She said good-bye to all the objects in her room.
"Goodbye to everything: I'll not return to this room!"
  She walked to the river, overcome by emotion,
Just like the ferryman who fell into the river.
She arranged her pair of red shoes on a rock,
And this chaste person jumped into the sea!

They called for her servant girl to come running;
Raising lamps in their hands, they raced about.
But searching the rooms to the east and the west,
They failed to find lady Luo in any of those places.
  They had killed a pig and a goat, prepared the wine,
As the sun brightly shone forth in the western sky.

8

THE MAIDEN MENG JIANG

VERSION 1

Transliterated and edited by Yi Nianhua and Zhou Shuoyi

The maiden Meng Jiang wept at the Long Wall—
For all eternity, a thousand years, her fame will endure.
  If you want to know why Meng Jiang acted this way,
Just listen, as I will tell you everything very clearly.
The maiden Jiang was born in the region of Youzhou;
Her father was known by the name Meng Nengren.
  The maiden Meng Jiang was his one and only child,
So she was not allowed to leave the house at will.
But for First Night of the First Month,[1]
She dressed up in all her finery to view the lanterns.
  She combed her hair, did it up in a coiled-dragon bun,
And she dressed herself in a dress of fresh new colors.
In her hair she had placed eight-jewel golden hairpins;
She looked just like Guansheyin of the southern ocean.[2]
  When she observed her face in the bright bronze mirror,
She truly was the most beautiful person in the world!

When she came out of the room and stepped forward,
She resembled an immortal maiden descending to earth.
  Ever since she had seen the First Night festival crowd,
Her passion was aroused and her love-longing stirred.
When she returned to her room, she thought to herself,
Thought to herself, "This year I've turned eighteen!
  Since earliest times an adult man takes a wife;
When a girl is grown up, she should marry a husband.
I'm afraid my parents are not paying any attention
And as yet have no intention to arrange my marriage!"

Let's not talk about Meng Jiang and her longings,
But let's turn our attention now to the king of Qin.
The king of Qin, fearing an invasion by others,
Wanted to build a myriad-mile wall in the east.
  This meant the people's star of disaster appeared:
It was the First Emperor, that ruler bereft of the Way!
He summoned the hundred officials to hear his orders;
He also summoned all the high officers in his court.
  That very day the First Emperor issued an edict:
Each region, prefecture, and county was to make known
That one man out of three was drafted, two out of five;
Money and grain were to be collected for these men.
  In Nanyang, in Dengzhou Prefecture, lived a Fan Changchun,
Whose family owned more than five hundred *mu* of good fields.
His only child was a son by the name of Fan Qilang,
A student who lived at home and studied the books.
  He was drafted as a laborer to work on the Great Wall,
And his family hired one replacement after another.
So when the district once again delivered a notice,
No money was left to hire another replacement.
  There was no other way than to go himself;
He prepared his luggage and set out on the journey.
After he had been in the Eastern Capital for more than a year,[3]
Not a penny was left of the ready cash he had brought.
  And so he had no alternative but to work hauling rice;
For each load he transported, he made five coppers.

How many heroes died in that way of exhaustion!
And how many fine young men died of starvation!
    Fan Qilang then thought to himself in his heart,
"If I continue this way, I'm bound to lose my life.
My best chance is to sneak away, flee for my life,
And return back home to continue the family line."
    He would have liked to travel over the broad open road
But feared he might be caught there by soldiers.
It would be better to take the small country roads;
On those small country roads it was easier to hide.
    If he traveled by daylight, people might spot him,
So he could walk on the road only during nighttime.
After he had traveled on for a number of nights,
He happened to arrive in Meng Family Village.
    In front of the Meng mansion was a lotus pond;
The lotus leaves in the pond provided protection.

At this time it happened to be the Sixth of the Sixth;
The grains in the fields promised a fine harvest.
Every family and household was filled with joy
And burned incense and paper to thank the gods.
    Nengren, who wanted to thank Heaven and Earth,
Ordered Meng Jiang to burn incense at the temple.
He ordered his daughter first to go to the pond
And purify her body before thanking the gods.
    When she received this order from her father,
Meng Jiang happily walked out onto the street.
When she arrived at the pond, she looked around:
Not a person was to be seen in whichever direction.
    Only after she had carefully looked all around her,
Only then did she start to take off her clothes.
She started by taking off her silk upper garment;
Next she took off her embroidered gauze skirt.
    The tender skin of her body a lotus-root white—
She was ready to step into the pond to bathe her body.
    Just as Meng Jiang stepped forward stark naked,
She all of a sudden discovered a student. No need

To tell of her panic as she hastily fled. Even that
Fan Qi was completely frightened out of his wits!

Meng Jiang promptly started to put on her clothes,
But as she put on her clothes, she watched the young man.
And while putting on her clothes, she told him,
She immediately told him to go meet her parents!

Fan Qilang, afraid that a policeman might arrive,
Had no option at all but to accompany her.

When the two of them arrived at the Meng mansion,
Nengren immediately asked, "Who is this guy?
Why did you try to rape my daughter at the pond?
We will definitely hand you over to the magistrate!"

Fan Qi was so scared that his heart jumped in his throat,
And he called out: "Dear sir, please let me explain!
My family lives in the Nanyang district in Qinzhou;[4]
My father is surnamed Fan and is quite well known.

It's the fault of the First Emperor, who, bereft of the Way,
Wants to build a myriad-mile wall at Chang'an.[5]

My family had a few hundred *mu* of fields,
But we sold them all to hire replacements for me.
When the county had yet another notice delivered,
There was, alas, no alternative but for me to go.

When I had gone and worked for more than a year,
Not a penny was left of the money I brought with me.
From then I had to rely on government rations:
Each man each day only got half a cup of rice.

How many heroes there died of exhaustion!
Watching such from nearby, my heart was broken!
That is the reason I took flight that very night,
And I only dared to walk on the roads at night.

When I came to the pond, I hid myself there;
Running into your daughter gave me quite a scare!
Dear sir, if you today are willing to pardon me,
I'll burn my flesh as incense to repay your grace!"

When Mr. Meng heard him speak like this, he
Realized this was someone to be pitied.

So he asked him this time: "How old are you now?
What are the year, month, and day of your birth?
    Do you or don't you already have a wife at home,
And what is your business? Please let me know!"
Fan Qi answered Mr. Meng in the following words:
"Dear sir, please allow me to provide an explanation.
    This year I am now eighteen years old, and I was
Born at noon on the first day of the Tenth Month.
At home I occupied myself by studying the books,
And since my youth I have not yet been engaged."
    Mr. Meng and his wife addressed him as follows:
"Young student, please accept our proposal.
You right now are eighteen years of age,
And of exactly the same age as our daughter.
    Since ancient times a girl at that age should marry,
And when a man turns eighteen, he should take a wife.
I will marry my daughter to you to be your wife
And ask Third Uncle to serve as the matchmaker."
    His wife replied, "You have spoken quite well;
The events of today really please my heart."
They invited Third Uncle to be the matchmaker
And treated relatives and neighbors to a banquet.
    When these guests had finished the wedding wine,
Meng Jiang and her husband entered the bridal chamber.
Husband and wife entered the red-gauze bed curtains:
A pair of mandarin ducks, joined together by Heaven!
    In the first watch: just like the phoenix seeking a mate,
Cooing together with a common tone of voice!
In the second watch: just like the Western Wing story,
They resembled Student Zhang wedding Yingying![6]
    In the third watch: just like the fishes playing in the stream,
They acted like the carps jumping across Dragon Gate!
In the fourth watch: just like a pair of turning millstones:
Mouth against mouth and heart against heart!
    In the fifth watch the Golden Rooster announced dawn,
And after only a little sleep the sky had turned bright!
One day turned to three, and three days turned to nine:

Husband and wife spent their time in happy harmony!
Mr. Meng and his wife, too, were filled with joy;
The whole household was enjoying this plenitude.
Who could know that misfortune soon was to strike,
And that a terrible disaster was about to befall?

The laborers building the wall all had fled;
Each region, prefecture, and county put up posters.
Those who were arrested counted in the millions;
Each one who was arrested substituted for two.
   The Meng mansion was visited by a ward leader
Who declared that Fan Qi was an escaped laborer.
He also went to the county to report his name, and
Two runners were dispatched to arrest their man.
   The two police runners arrived in great haste;
Once they arrested Fan Qi, they set out to depart.
Meng Jiang stepped forward and in a friendly way said,
"Dear officers, please do not be in such a hurry!

I have golden hairpins, which weigh three ounces;
I also have here twenty ounces of finest silver.
Since ancient times enlightened officials do good;
Whenever they can spare a man, they'll spare him."
   The two runners replied to her words as follows:
"We police officers have to be very circumspect;
We would not dare demand your gold and silver!
Please ready his luggage quickly so we may go!"
   Meng Jiang at that moment fainted and collapsed,
And her two elderly parents were awash in tears.
Fan Qilang hastily helped his wife to her feet again,
And a recovered Meng Jiang sent her husband off.
   She saw her husband off for one mile, coming to the gate,
All the while stamping her feet and beating her breast.
"I'd hoped that husband and wife would stay together forever.
Who could have known this flower would bloom in vain?"
   She saw her husband off for two miles, passing by the gate,
And a pair of mandarin ducks took wing and flew off.
"When mandarin ducks take wing, they fly a thousand miles;

They only long to be a couple, refusing to be separated!"
    She saw her husband off for three miles, to the pavilion;
She led Fan Qi by the hand, had him accept a jacket-front.
"I give these two pieces making up a jacket-front to you—
It is so easy to see you off, but so hard to see you again!"
    She saw her husband off for four miles, to a field,
And as she looked at the field, her tears coursed down.
"I will sow the seeds of the five grains in this field,
But if the field lacks water, they will not grow!"
    She saw her husband of for five miles, to a bridge,
Both of them, hand in hand, watched the water flow.
"Never be like the water below the bridge, as it only
Flows off toward the eastern sea and never returns!"
    She saw her husband off for six miles, to a pond;
The wind on the lotus leaves spread their fragrance.
"Because of roots and leaves the flowers bear fruit;
Without roots and leaves they'd not form a couple."
    She saw her husband off to the seven-mile rapids,
Reminding her of Weaving Girl and Buffalo Herder.
"Never be like Buffalo Herder and Weaving Girl—
Husband and wife for eternity, but forever divorced!"[7]
    She saw her husband off for eight miles, to a garden,
She saw the bright flowers, and her tears coursed down.
"Flowers bloom and flowers fade, every year anew,
But human beings are unable to regain their youth!"
    She saw her husband off for nine miles, across a hill,
And wildflowers were blooming all over that hill.
"My husband, never pluck wildflowers on a hill,
Because if you do, you'll be breaking my heart!"[8]
    She saw her husband off for ten miles, to a dike,
Where she gave her gold and silver to her husband.
She also implored his escorts in a friendly manner
To take good care of Fan Qi, "my darling husband!"

Let's not talk about Meng Jiang seeing her husband off;
Let's speak of Fan Qi, arriving in the Eastern Capital.
As soon as his commanding officer saw Fan Qi return,

He gnashed his teeth, and repeatedly cursed him.
　As a greeting he gave him thirty strokes of the rod;
Afterward he had him taken to the jail and locked up.
Alas, Fan Qi had no food or drink for three days,
And he died there in the jail of hunger and starvation.
　As nobody came and claimed his body for burial,
His bones were dumped inside the myriad-mile wall.

Let's not go on about Fan Qi's return to the shades,
But let's return again to the subject of Meng Jiang.
Ever since her separation from her darling husband,
She waited at home every day for his return.
　In the First Month, one of longing, it was the New Year!
"Lanterns of glass are hung up in front of the hall.
Others families now all are drinking New Year wine,
But it's only my Fan Qi who is far away from here."
　In the Second Month all the flowers were blooming!
"I'm just like Zhao Wuniang longing for Cai Yong.[9]
The swallows on the rafters know to come and go;
It is only my husband I do not see coming back home."
　In the Third Month it was the time of Clear and Bright.
"Every family and household goes out to sweep the graves.
All other people sweep the graves with their husbands,
But it is only I, Meng Jiang, who has to walk alone."
　The Fourth Month is the season for picking mulberry leaves,
And Meng Jiang went out alone to pick mulberry leaves.
"My hand grabs the branches, but I don't pick the leaves,
As my heart is occupied with longing for my Fan Qilang."
　In the Fifth Month people celebrate Double-Fifth;
On the racing boats the beaten drums roar and rumble.
"Other people now all drink their Double-Fifth wine,
But I still don't see my Fan Qilang coming back home."
　In the Sixth Month it was again the feast of Double-Sixth;
Last year on this same day she had found her husband.
"When I think back to the day of our first meeting,
I cannot stop myself from weeping as he still is not back!"
　In the Seventh Month people celebrate Middle Prime.

"Every family and household welcomes its ancestors home.[10]
Your wife here has been waiting for you past the fifteenth;
Out of longing for my Fan Qi, my tears keep on flowing."

In the Eighth Month people celebrate Mid-Autumn.
"The moon is fully rounded, yet I'm filled with sorrow;
My Fan Qilang is far away, and I never got any letter;
My longing for my absent husband increases my grief."

In the Ninth Month people celebrate Double-Ninth.
"I'm just like Li Sanniang longing for Liu Zhiyuan.[11]
In other homes husband and wife drink wine together,
But my husband is staying in a region far away."

In the Tenth Month it was the Beginning of Winter.
"Without karmic cause man and wife don't come together.
Can it be that in a former life I did not practice virtue,
And that now I am in the west and he is in the east?"

In the month of winter the snowflakes swirled about;
Her longing for her husband was wrecking her heart.
"Despite the cold weather my husband is still not back;
I'd like to go and find him, but the journey is so far!"

In the Last Month she yearned for him till New Year's Eve.
"All year long I have been waiting and watching.
All other families now drink New Year's Eve wine,
But Fan Qilang and I still are not together again."

She waited for him for a year, and then another year:
In this life husband and wife were never complete.
All day long she longed for her husband, each day!
In her room by herself her tears coursed down.

After she had considered the case from all directions,
She decided to go to the capital to find her husband.
So Meng Jiang addressed her parents as follows:
"I will go and travel in person to Chang'an!

And because the weather is so terribly cold,
I will take my husband an extra set of clothes."

Her parents in the hall answered her as follows:
"My child, please listen to what we have to say.
You are only a woman, so how would you be able

To travel all by yourself to such a faraway place?"
  Meng Jiang addressed her parents once more:
"Your daughter really has made up her mind!
A good woman can enter a crowd of a thousand men;
She doesn't fear the other party, more than a myriad!
  But because of my love for my husband,
I am not afraid of high mountains or long roads.
When I find my husband, we'll come back here together,
And I'll leave a lasting reputation for all eternity.
  If something or another untoward happens,
I can stand a myriad cuts or a thousand wounds.
Here in front of my parents I make the vow that I
Will not return home until I have found my man!"

She took her leave of her parents and left,
Crossing rivers and mountains to seek her husband.
Holding a lute in her hands, she walked in front;
Her servant girl followed, carrying the luggage.
  She crossed thousands and thousands of mountains;
She crossed thousands and thousands of rivers.
She suffered endless hardship on her journey;
Seeking her husband, she arrived at the Great Wall.
  Seeking here and there, she did not find him,
And unexpectedly she arrived at a temple,
Where she asked the priest to tell her fortune.
Her question was where to find her husband.
  The priest replied to her in the following words:
"This hexagram I obtained is not very lucky.
It is hard to tell you the hexagram's message:
Most likely he's dead and will not revive!"
  When Meng Jiang heard these words from the priest,
She burst into tears and could not stop crying.
She went to the office of his commanding officer,
And she asked him for her husband, Fan Qilang.
  He replied to her, "Indeed, we had a Fan Qilang;
Last year he was killed on the execution ground.
Because nobody claimed his bones for burial,

We then buried him in the myriad-mile wall."
    When Meng Jiang heard this, she wept loudly,
Weeping and wailing in a most saddening way.
She wept for three days, and then for three nights,
Moved Heaven and Earth, and crumbled the wall!
    Meng Jiang recovered her husband's bones;
She carried them home and put them in her room.
Each night she slept alongside her husband's bones,
And never in her life did she marry another man.

This is the end of the story of the maiden Meng Jiang,
Who left a fine reputation that will last through eternity.

VERSION 2

Written out by Yi Nianhua

On the sixth of the Sixth Month the heat is too much:
The sun resembles a fire, rivers seem to be boiling!
The maiden Jiang stepped into the rear flower garden;
She quickly took off her clothes and got into the pond.
    Her shift and skirt she had hung on a willow tree;
She lightly splattered water, sprinkling mandarin ducks.
After splashing the mandarin ducks, she turned around
And saw a man who was hiding in a mulberry tree.
    The maiden Jiang hastily grabbed her shift and skirt;
She grabbed her shift and skirt and put them on.
Layer upon layer she dressed herself properly.[12]
    Once she was dressed again, she questioned him,
Asking, "Where are you from, from which county?
Where does your family live, and in which county?
What is your family name, and where do you live?"
    Fan Lang replied to her in the following manner:
"Young lady, please listen to what I have to say.
    I am from a different prefecture, a different county,
As I live within the walls of the city of Chang'an;

The only child of my parents, it was just us three,
So I was drafted to dig clay and lay bricks for the wall.
    I, Fan Lang, am still young, only fifteen years old;
Each day and each night I spent in my study.
Give me paper and brush, and I can write an essay,
But I cannot dig clay and I cannot lay bricks.
    By day we had to dig clay, by night lay bricks;
That terrible hardship was more than I could bear."
    The young lady answered the young man as follows:
"Young man, please listen to what I have to say.
If you, Fan Lang, will climb down from that tree,
We will be married as husband and wife forever.
    But if you, Fan Lang, refuse to come down from that tree,
We will draft a statement and send you to the magistrate.
When we send you off to appear before the magistrate,
We will say you are an escaped laborer from Chang'an."
    The young man answered the young lady as follows:
"Young lady, please listen to what I have to say.
A thousand miles, yet one's karma will cause a meeting;
A myriad of miles, yet one's karma will create a couple."

The maiden Jiang pondered this matter in her heart,
And she immediately led her husband into the hall:
"Today I happened to meet with young master Fan;
Disregarding my parents' wishes, I acted on my own."
    The maiden Jiang led her husband into the hall;
Of one mind the two of them bowed before her parents.
The maiden Jiang led her husband into her private room;
Amid the bridal room's flowers, candles shed their light.
    A pearly red-gauze skirt and thin silk bed curtains,
Clear lamps darkly displayed the ivory-inlaid couch.
Once on the dragon-couch, a couple of mandarin ducks—
"All my heart and all my loving feelings I give to you!"
    When the drum sounded the third watch at midnight,
Three times they shouted: "We come to arrest Fan Lang!"
The maiden Jiang hastily opened her chests
To dispense a great quantity of gold and silver.

"That quantity of gold and silver we do not want;
We are police officers under the strictest of orders."
Such a fine red flower—Fan Lang was arrested.
Find a flower—it falls to the ground, who . . .

    That one night for one night they were like dew and water;
Before the five watches were over, the sky had dawned.
The maiden Jiang saw her husband off for some miles,
And she wept so much her face was awash in tears.

In the First Month, one of longing, it was the New Year!
"Lanterns of glass are hung in front of the hall."
In the Second Month all the flowers were blooming!

    In the Third Month it was the time of Clear and Bright.
"Every family and household goes out to sweep the graves.
All other people have husbands, follow their husbands,
But it is only I, Meng Jiang, who has to go alone."

    The Fourth Month is the beginning of summer.
"Brother and sister are out picking mulberry leaves.
My hand bends the branches but I don't pick the leaves,
As my heart is filled with longing for my Fan Qilang."

    In the Fifth Month people celebrate Double-Fifth;
On the racing boats the beaten drums roar and rumble.
In the Sixth Month it was again the feast of Double-Sixth.
"Last year on this same day we became husband and wife."

    In the Seventh Month people welcome the ancestors home.
"My husband did not return to spend the fifteenth here;
I keep to my room, and my tears keep on flowing."

    In the Eighth Month people celebrate Mid-Autumn.
"By the light of the moon I am filled with sorrow."
In the Ninth Month people celebrate Double-Ninth.
"My husband is not at home to celebrate Double-Ninth."

    In the Tenth Month it was the Beginning of Winter.
"May Kongming on his terrace conjure up the east wind,
An east wind that, once conjured up, howls and roars—
All because my husband does not return home."[13]

    In the Eleventh Month the snowflakes swirled about,
And the young girl Meng Jiang delivered winter clothes,

Delivered them to the Great Wall—thirty thousand miles!
But she did not see her husband—how heartrending.

In the Twelfth Month she longed for him till New Year's Eve;
She waited for him for a year, and then another year.
She waited for him for a year, and then another year—
"All because my husband does not return home."

9

THE FLOWER SELLER

Originally transcribed by Hu Cizhu; written out again

by Gao Yinxian and Yi Nianhua

All those many other idle words I will not sing at all,
But let me sing about someone from Henan Province.
In Henan Province one finds the prefecture of Kaifeng,
And in the county of Antong there was a small town.

    Renowned for generations, that was millionaire Liu;
His wife was ennobled as a Lady by imperial patent.
The couple, husband and wife, did many good deeds,
And they had three children, all of them being sons!

    The three sons went to school and learned their letters,
But despite their many attempts, they never succeeded.
Once they had given their situation long and hard thought,
The brothers became merchants, people engaged in trade.

    The eldest brother in Tongzhou bought mules and horses,
But he died in Tongzhou and never made the trip home.
The second brother became a trader on rivers and lakes,
But he died on the rivers and lakes and went to the shades.

    This left only the third brother, who was still so young;
He was sent to school where he studied the Five Classics.
The name that was chosen for him was Liu Sijun,
And to the end of his long life that name was not changed.

He studied from the age of seven till the age of fifteen,
So he might succeed as the top of the list, the number one!
The woman he married was a daughter of the Zhang family,
And husband and wife spent their days living together.

    Now this lady Zhang was extremely filial and obedient;
She filially served her parents-in-law, the elderly couple.

But let's not talk of lady Zhang's great filial obedience—
The Decree of Heaven does not keep the elderly alive.
The life of magnate Liu returned to the realm of the shades;
On earth he left behind the Lady, and his son and his wife.

    In one year they suffered three times from a huge fire;
In three years they were nine times accused of homicide.
Their boats that were plying the lakes all went down,
And all of their servants and boys deserted them and fled.

    Their thirteen shop fronts were all without tenants,
And not a single servant guarded their gate anymore.
And as if the family had not suffered setbacks enough,
On top of that they then encountered their archenemy!

    In Henan Province arrived a certain prefect Wang,
Who wanted us to transport grain to the city of Nanjing![1]
Transporting one hundred twenty thousand *liang* of silver,
Liu arrived at Raven River and there ran into disaster.

    Whereas earlier they had a bright sky and blazing sun,
They suddenly were surprised by the arrival of a twister.
The full amount of the money was completely lost,
And twenty of the family's servants died by drowning.

    The only person to be saved was young master Liu;
Holding onto a mast pole, he loudly cried out for help.

    The astral lord of Great White descended to earth,
And rowing a little boat he arrived on the scene.
Quickly he saved young master Liu from the water
And then took him to safety on the southern shore.

The young master could only loudly weep and cry;
He did not have any money with which to travel back home.
After long and hard thinking he saw no other solution

But to make the trip back home by begging all the way.

Sleeping under the stars, he suffered many hardships;
He suffered a thousand kinds of myriads of hardships.
When eventually one day he arrived back home again,
His tears coursed down and fell in great profusion.

His lovely wife came out of her room to welcome him;
She offered him a cup of tea, saying, "My dear husband,
What is the reason for your sorrow on your return home?
Please tell your wife everything, from the very beginning."

The young master promptly addressed her as follows:
"My dear wife, how could you know what has happened?

When I left some time ago to transport grain to Nanjing,
The boat sank in a storm, and then everything was gone!
Twenty of the family's servants died by drowning,
And I made the trip back home by begging all the way."

When the young lady heard this, tears coursed down,
And again and again she cried out, "My dear husband!
Fields and farms, money and goods are like cold water;
Only a post in the Hanlin Academy is worth a million.²

Gold and silver, jewels and pearls are bland like water;
The only thing that counts is that you have been saved."
They immediately sold all of their fields and farms,
So as to take a replacement shipment again to Nanjing.

Once they had made up for the one hundred twenty thousand,
They had sold off all of their possessions, large and small;
He, his wife, and his mother, three in all, had no place to live,
So they went and took shelter in a dilapidated kiln.

During the day they had no money at all and no rice;
At night they had not a single sheet to cover their bodies.
So the young lady stepped forward and spoke as follows:
"My dear husband, please listen to what I have to say.

In my opinion we cannot just resign ourselves to fate!
I will go out on the streets and become a flower seller.
I will cut flowers out of paper and sell them on the streets,
Hoping in this way to make some money so we can survive."

When the young master heard this, he spoke as follows:

"My dear wife, now please listen to what I have to say.
It would be better if you stayed at home, doing nothing—
Never become a woman who shows her face in public."

The young lady did not listen to her husband's words,
But she went to her mother-in-law, that elderly woman.

"Our family's fortune has met with very hard times;
Our family's wealth of millions has all been sold off.
To no avail we are suffering hunger in this old kiln,
With no grain of rice in the house it is hard to survive.

I, your daughter-in-law, have been thinking I might
Cut paper flowers and go sell them to make money.
I think I will go and hawk them on the main streets;
I will sell them for money and rice so we may survive."

When her mother heard this, her tears coursed down,
And again and again she called out, "My dear daughter,
You are the precious daughter of a family of officials—
How could you become someone who sells flowers?"

The young lady addressed her once more, as follows:
"My dear mother-in-law, please listen to what I say.
I've been told that the ancients had a saying that goes:
'A family's slide into poverty is not a personal fault.'"

She thereupon took a pair of scissors in her hand
And cut out paper flowers that were oh so lovely:
First she cut out peony flowers with green leaves;
Her lotus and crabapple flowers were true to life.

Once she had cut out a hundred pairs of flowers,
She went off to the Eastern Capital with her basket.[3]
She walked from the eastern to the western streets;
She walked from the southern to the northern streets.

The older and younger men all came and stared at her;
Each and every one stared at this flower-selling woman.
As soon as she noticed this, she was filled with rage.
"You gentlemen all, please listen to what I have to say.

Everybody has his own elder and younger sisters;
Each of you has his own sisters who go outdoors.
If you goggle at the wives and daughters of others,
Your wife and daughter will be raped by others."

Before she had even finished making her speech,
All of these men, old and young, went back home.

I'll not sing of all the men who had returned home;
I'll sing again of this one woman selling flowers.
    Carrying her flower basket, she called for customers.
"Alas, alas, Old Man Heaven is so utterly unfair!
In earlier days our family possessed tens of millions.
Who'd have known we would now end up so poor!"
    Just as the young lady was crying her heart out,
The astral lord of Great White descended to the earth.
The astral lord of Great White transformed himself,
Transformed himself into a local vegetable peddler.
    He hastily put down his carrying pole and said:
"You, woman selling flowers, please listen to me!
    The eastern and western streets—there you can go,
But never go inside the mansion of the Cao family.
That Cao is the father-in-law of Emperor Renzong;
He forces ordinary women to become his concubines!"
    The young lady immediately replied as follows:
"Granddad, what you are saying makes no sense at all!
All I do is sell my flowers out here in the street.
What do I care for any relative of the imperial house?"

Walking ahead, she passed in front of the Cao mansion
Just as the emperor's father-in-law was at the gate.
When she arrived outside the gate of the mansion,
He saw and noticed that one woman selling flowers.
    As she was holding a pair of flowers in her hand,
Her perfect beauty was utterly stunning, oh so lovely!
Her three-inch golden lotuses were extremely small,
Driving the emperor's father-in-law crazy with lust.
    "I have a wife and concubines, nine women in all,
But they don't measure up to half of this woman.
If I could only share the bed curtains with this woman,
I will not have lived my current existence in vain!"
    He hastily ordered two of the men under his command

To go and catch that woman who was selling flowers.
　　The two men immediately took off, running in a hurry,
Until they found her in the street and walked up to her.
The two of them stepped forward and said repeatedly,
"You, woman who is peddling flowers, please listen!
The young lady at our mansion is sending for you,
And she is asking you to follow us to the mansion."

The woman did not realize their true intentions;
She didn't know she would be entering the gate of disaster.
When she arrived at the mansion after a while,
She saw a pair of golden lions guarding the gate.
　　On reaching the second gate of the Cao mansion,
She saw two soaring phoenixes flying into the gate.
And when she reached the third gate straight ahead,
Lances, swords, and axes were seen on both sides.
　　When she then reached the fourth gate further on,
Serving maids in pairs were arranged on both sides.
But when she then reached the fifth gate further on,
It was one crowd of tiger tallies and battle flags.
　　When she reached the sixth gate yet further on,
Bright golden lamps were shedding their light.
But when she reached the seventh gate yet further on,
She didn't see the young lady anywhere around!
　　The emperor's father-in-law was seated there,
The authority he displayed truly awe inspiring!
He promptly addressed this question to lady Zhang:
"What kind of money do you ask for those flowers?"
　　Lady Zhang immediately answered as follows:
"Your Excellency, please listen to what I have to say.
The big flowers sell for eight *fen* of silver a pair;
The small flowers go for six *fen* of silver a pair."
　　The emperor's father-in-law laughed heartily.
"My dear woman, you clearly don't get the message!
The gold and silver here is more than can be carried.
Who here cares for those paper flowers of yours?
　　But since you have come and arrived in my house,

Allow me, dear woman, to ask, where are you from?
In which prefecture, in which county do you live?
And how did you become a flower-selling woman?"
  The woman immediately answered as follows:
"I am from Kaifeng Prefecture in Henan Province.
If Your Excellency doesn't want to buy my flowers,
Why did you invite me into this mansion of yours?"

The emperor's father-in-law laughed heartily
And called out to her, "My dear young woman,
Your figure is fine and your beauty is stunning.
And now you are trapped in my mighty mansion!
  Of course I have wives, nine women in total,
But I am still short of consort number ten.
If you, dear woman, comply with my wishes,
You'll eat only lamb and the finest delicacies.
  For your hair you'll have pearls and precious gems,
Your body—wrapped in silks and brocade gowns.
When you go out, your equipage will be oh so grand,
And servant girls will be following you at all times."
  When the woman heard this, she promptly answered,
"Your Excellency, what you propose makes no sense.
  The matter is that I am already a married woman,
And I have a little boy who is three years of age.[4]
You are one of the highest officials of the court.
How could you be without fitting women as partners?
  Dragon paired to dragon, phoenix paired to phoenix—
How could a poor creature like me dare marry you?
In this matter I am unable to comply with your wish;
May Your Excellency be so kind as to let me go home."
  The emperor's father-in-law addressed her once more,
Saying, "Dear woman, do not stick to these formalities!
What does marriage have to do with poverty or wealth?
Noble and base as settled by Heaven unite in wedlock.
  Dear woman, if you agree to comply with my wishes,
You'll be put in charge of all the affairs of my house.
But if you disobey me for as little as half a sentence,

You'll be unable to escape from this mansion today!"
    Hearing this, the young lady Zhang was filled with rage,
And she loudly cursed His Excellency for being evil.
    "Your son-in-law at court may be the Son of Heaven,
But the royal laws don't take relatives into account.
I should report the matter to the golden palace hall
In order to ensure that you will not live to old age!"
    Then the emperor's father-in-law was filled with rage
And cursed her a number of times. "You brazen slut!
Apart from His Majesty, I'm the most powerful person.
Please be so kind as to report this matter to the Throne!
    If you here and now quickly comply with my wishes,
We'll leave the matter as it is and not pursue it further.
If you indicate your refusal with only half a sentence,
The steel swords in this mansion will grant no pardon!"
    Lady Zhang answered him again in the following words,
Saying, "Your Excellency, be so kind as to listen well.
    A good horse will not carry a couple of saddles;
A good woman will not marry two husbands in a row.
If a horse carries two saddles, it is difficult to travel;
If a woman marries two husbands, she's cursed by all.
    I would rather be the ghost of one killed by a sword
Than lose my honor by marrying Your Excellency!
If I would agree to a marriage to Your Excellency,
I'd have fur and horns—because I would be a beast!"

As soon as His Excellency heard her say this word,
It called up one basin of raging fire in his heart, and
He ordered the men under his command to take action
And beat this foxy witch to death as soon as possible!
    Those to his left and right, up and down, raced forward,
All of these men looking like wolves and like tigers.
They shackled that flower-selling woman, lady Zhang,
And dragged her out through three gates of the mansion.
    The pressing boards, the bamboo splints,[5] endless shouts:
Lady Zhang already had lost two of her three souls, so
She cried out, "Dear lords, please, please spare my life;

I'll repay your grace by cutting flesh, burning incense!"

All of his underlings answered her in the following way:
"His Excellency does not want to be your archenemy.
We only urge you to comply with his wish in this matter,
So you won't have to meet with King Yama this very day."

The emperor's father-in-law promptly gave the order
That not the slightest delay was allowed, not a second!
As soon as they heard this, his underling took action;
By one hand they dragged her out of his presence.

They tied her up in the biggest hall of the house;
Lady Zhang's tears coursed down as she loudly wept,

"For me it is only a minor matter to be killed here,
But on whom will my three-year-old baby boy rely?
My elderly mother-in-law will have none to serve her,
And I'll leave my husband behind, desolate and alone."

The young lady cried for mercy as loud as she could,
But these evil-minded underlings showed no compassion.
Each hit of the bronze hammer weighed three pounds.
Three hits of the bronze hammer weighed nine pounds.

She was beaten with bronze hammers, left and right:
Her whole body was beaten into one bloody pulp.

Lady Zhang was the daughter of a family of officials;
She never in her life had suffered such terrible torture.
The blood flowed from her seven arteries, and she died,
Becoming a traveler on the road to the Yellow Springs.[6]

The emperor's father-in-law immediately ordered
That she be buried in the flower garden to the west.
Her body was placed in a deep hole in the ground,
And then it was covered with a heavy slab of stone.

On top of that slab of stone they deposited earth,
One layer of earth, and then one layer of bricks.
A bronze nail was hammered through her mouth,
So her family would never have any descendants.

At the head of her grave narcissuses were planted,
And at the bottom they planted some crabapple trees.

In between they planted some banana trees, so she
Would not be able to turn over for all eternity.

Let's not sing of lady Zhang and the way she died;
Let's sing once again of her husband, that Liu Sijun.
Back at home all day long he waited for her return,
But even at night lady Zhang had still not returned.
     When their three-year-old darling baby started to cry,
Sijun said to his mother, "Could your daughter-in-law
Perhaps have had a change of heart—have turned into
One of those who despise poverty and love riches?"
     The mother promptly answered her son as follows:
"You wife, I would think, is not that kind of person.
It must be because the main street is very far away;
I am quite sure that tomorrow she'll be back home."

Let's not sing of the three of them waiting in the kiln,
But let's sing of that wronged flower-selling woman.
     After the young lady Zhang had died, she arrived
Below the Nine Springs at the underworld courts.[7]
Before her wronged soul arrived in front of King Yama,
She saw all ten kings of the underworld courts.
     Once King Yama had looked into her case, he found
That lady Zhang was a ghost who had suffered injustice.
"This is one who died wrongly in the world of light,
So send her back to earth so she may right this wrong!"
     As soon as lady Zhang heard this, she hastily ran off;
As a gust of black wind she quickly made the trip.

Lady Zhang's wronged soul arrived without delay;
Weeping and crying, she arrived at the kiln at midnight.
     She only called out to her husband and said to him,
"Look at you, sleeping so soundly in your dreams!
Yesterday your wife went off to the Eastern Capital;
I went there to sell my flowers on the city's streets.
     Could I have known that when I passed the Cao mansion,

I would happen to run into the emperor's father-in-law?
As soon as he saw the beauty of my features,
He pressured me to become one of his many concubines.

When I refused to comply, he had me beaten to death
And buried in the flower garden on the western side.
They dug a hole in the earth to a depth of two *zhang*:
One layer of earth, and then one layer of stones.

At the head of the grave narcissuses were planted;
At the bottom they planted some crabapple trees.
In the middle they planted some banana trees,
So I would not be able to turn over for all eternity.

I now have come back to send you this dream, please
Remember the one who shared your cushion and couch!
Judge Bao of Kaifeng Prefecture is as clear as water:
During the day he judges on earth, at night with the shades!

There are so many other things that I would like to say,
But I already hear the Golden Rooster announcing the dawn."

A crying and weeping lady Zhang had sent him a dream,
So now let's sing of Liu Sijun, the one who saw the dream.
"In my dream I saw my dear wife all awash in tears;
I'm so scared that my clothes are wet with cold sweat.

That's why I have been calling for you again and again;
My dear mother, I dreamt of your daughter-in-law.
She spoke to me in a clear and unmistakable voice
And looked exactly as she used to, and she told me

She was beaten to death by the emperor's father-in-law
And had been buried in the garden on the western side.
She then ordered me to go to the prefecture of Kaifeng
And plead with the prefect Judge Bao to right her wrong."

His mother answered her son in the following manner:
"The words one hears in a dream are not always true.

Thoughts that haunt one during the day turn to dreams.
The proverb goes: 'Who dies in a dream may yet live.'
Wait for the light of dawn, then go and investigate,
Investigate the truth of the matter, for better or worse."

When Liu Sijun had heard these words from his mother,

He left to look for his wife before the sky was bright.
And once he arrived inside the city of Kaifeng,
He searched for his wife in all directions on the streets.

From eastern streets to western streets he searched;
From southern streets to northern streets he walked.
Whenever he met with a man, he questioned that man;
Whenever he ran into someone, he questioned that person.

They all told him that a woman who was selling flowers
Had come to the gate of the Cao family's mansion.
"And not just this one woman who was selling flowers,
Even ten of them would not have been able to return!"

When Liu Sijun heard these people talk in this way,
It was clear that the words in the dream had been true!
He immediately ran to the station that licensed peddlers
To discuss with its director how to right this wrong!

Let's drop the subject of Sijun, not talk about him—
Let's sing once again of the emperor's father-in-law.
As His Excellency was seated in the biggest hall,
His heart was beset by worries, he was not at ease.

He knew too well that the death of this flower peddler
Was a wrong and an injustice that had not been cleared.
So he ordered his underlings to ready his sedan chair:
He wanted to burn incense and venerate all the gods.

Let's not sing of the emperor's father-in-law, on his way
To burn incense—let's sing once again of Liu Sijun.

He took the man who arrived to be Clear-Sky Judge Bao,
So he immediately shouted, "Please hear my plea!"
He knelt down on both knees and wept without end,
"Your Excellency Clear-Sky, please right my wrong!

I report to you a wrong and injustice I have suffered,
Hoping Your Excellency will give a clear verdict!
The man I now accuse of this crime is none other
Than the emperor's father-in-law—that's the one I accuse."

Sir Cao first accepted the written accusation to look at it,
Then ordered his underlings to arrest Liu Sijun and said,

"You brazen scoundrel, I am entitled to curse you,
As I here and now am that emperor's father-in-law!
      Today it is not me who came to search for you—
Like a moth flying into the flame, burning his body."

His underlings dragged Liu Sijun to the big hall of the house;
One shout from them was enough to scare one to death!
      Sir Cao threw down a bamboo slip for a full forty strokes—
Liu Sijun's skin was ripped from his buttocks by that beating!
Following that beating they applied the pressing boards
Again and again, then threw him into the water-prison.
      As the young master was sitting in the water-prison,
[He thought,] "My chance of survival is one out of ten!
My wife has been beaten to death by that bastard,
And now it's my turn to die here in his water-prison."

The ghost of lady Zhang came to this water-prison
And called out, "My dear husband, I told you so clearly
      To go to Kaifeng Prefecture to lodge your accusation,
But you had to run into your archenemy, of all people!
Now you stay in this water-prison and persevere,
While I go off to Kaifeng Prefecture to right this wrong!"

As Judge Bao took his seat behind the bench in the hall,
A gust of black wind arrived before him, so Judge Bao,
As soon as he saw it, called out in that booming voice,
"Wronged ghost from where you may be, now speak up!"
      Lady Zhang then knelt down on both knees, saying,
"Clear-Sky Judge Bao, please listen and right my wrong!
      As to my own name, I am a daughter of the Zhang family;
The husband I was married to is called Liu Sijun.
Because we had become so poor we couldn't survive,
I cut out paper flowers to sell for dimes and cents.
      By chance I passed in front of the mansion of Sir Cao,
And I was pressured to become one of his concubines.
When I refused to comply with his wishes, I was killed
And buried in the flower garden on the western side.

They dug a hole in the earth to a depth of two *zhang*:
One layer of earth, and then one layer of stones.
At the head of the grave narcissuses were planted;
At the bottom they planted some crabapple trees.
In the middle they planted some banana trees,
So I would not be able to turn over for all eternity.

Through my mouth they hammered a bronze nail;
In the world of shade I reported this to King Yama.
He ordered me to return to earth and lodge a complaint;
Weeping and crying, I arrived at midnight at the kiln.

I sent a dream to my husband sleeping on his bed,
Telling him to appeal for justice to Your Excellency.
Who could have known he would meet with Sir Cao?
My husband ran into his archenemy, of all people!

Without listening to any explanation, Sir Cao had him beaten,
And then my husband was thrown into the water-prison!
Again I hope that Your Excellency will hear our case
And give a clear verdict in a feud of a river of blood!"

As soon as Judge Bao had heard this wronged ghost,
He loudly cursed the emperor's father-in-law as evil.

That very moment Judge Bao came up with a plan,
And taking out paper and brush, he composed a letter.
First he wrote "Bao Wenzheng of the Southern Office[8]
Greets His Excellency, the emperor's father-in-law.

As I, your student, have distributed grain in Chenzhou,[9]
My heart is filled with worries; I am lacking in energy.
I have heard about the beauty of your flower gardens,
So a short visit to your place would relieve my spirit."

As soon as Judge Bao finished writing this letter,
He handed it to his servants Zhang Long and Zhao Hu.
As soon as these two persons received this letter,
They went and delivered it to His Excellency Cao.

When the emperor's father-in-law read this letter,
He was pretty sure what was behind this little note.

"This must be because of that woman selling flowers;

The wrong that I've done her has come back to haunt me!
But if that Judge Bao wants to have a look at the garden,
I will welcome Judge Bao and let him have his look.

You're free to look at the eastern and southern gardens,
You're free to walk through the northern flower garden,
But the flower garden to the west will be locked up,
And the lock will be sealed with any number of seals!"

Immediately Sir Cao composed a letter in reply,
Which he handed to the two servants Zhang and Zhao:
"If your master wants to relieve his mind and spirit,
I'll be happy to let him come and look at his leisure."

The two servants immediately returned back home
And informed Judge Bao of what Sir Cao had said.
Hearing this, Judge Bao hastily prepared himself
And set out with a complete escort of armed soldiers.

Let's not sing of Judge Bao, who set out on his way,
But let's sing again of the emperor's father-in-law.
He set out a banquet in the eastern flower garden;
The lamb and the wine were of the finest quality!

The music of pipes and drums resounded loudly—
One layer of soldiers, and then one layer of servants!
One pair of swords of steel for every pair of axes:
The troops and their officers filled one with fear!

Once the Cao mansion had made its arrangements,
It welcomed His Excellency Bao, the city prefect.
When Judge Bao thereupon arrived in the high hall,
Two masters of ceremony guided him to his seat.

After a cup of tea Judge Bao spoke as follows:
"I, your student, have lately been lacking in spirit.
I've heard about the beauty of your flower gardens,
And a short visit would really relieve my mind."

The emperor's father-in-law said, "That's fine!"
Together they walked about in the flower garden.
A banquet had been spread there in the flower garden,
And seated opposite each other, they drank their wine.

After Judge Bao had finished drinking his wine,

He walked all around through the flower gardens.
He looked all over, but no place fit the description,
So he addressed the emperor's father-in-law, saying,

"People all say that your flower gardens are beautiful,
And that reputation is not empty—it is indeed the truth.
I've seen the eastern garden and the northern garden,
So now I would also like to see the western courtyard."

Sir Cao immediately came up with an excuse and said,
"Your Excellency Bao, I'm very much afraid that, alas,
It will be impossible for you to see the western garden,
Because that is the quarters of my wife and the girls."

Judge Bao immediately answered him as follows:
"Don't tell me that your wife lives in the western garden!
Even if it was Her Majesty the emperor's main consort,
I still would want to take a stroll through that garden!"

He ordered his servants Zhang Long and Zhao Hu
To open the two wings of the western garden's gate.
And as soon as Judge Bao threw a look into that garden,
He noticed a spot newly planted with flowers and trees.

The new plants and trees were indeed of three kinds,
Exactly as had been told to him by the wronged ghost.

Judge Bao then said to the emperor's father-in-law,
"The beauty of your flower gardens is truly stunning!
The narcissuses, that crabapple, that banana tree:
Below those three flowers a bright light is shining!

A few days ago I was told in a dream that a treasure
Of gold and silver was hidden under these flowers.
Now let's order our servants to dig that treasure up,
And you and I will divide fairly whatever is found!"

When the emperor's father-in-law heard these words,
He seemed as if doused with a bucket of ice-cold water.
But Zhang Long and Zhao Hu wasted not a moment and
Started to dig with their hoes, without showing mercy.

From early morning till noon they went on digging:
One layer of flat stones, and then a layer of bricks.

They dug through the flat stones, dug through the earth,
And by digging through the earth discovered the corpse.

As soon as Judge Bao saw that this was the woman,
He loudly cursed the emperor's father-in-law, saying,
    "You have been showered with favors by the court,
And here in the city of Kaifeng you commit murder!
Today you have broken the nation's laws by the book;
Even the king's own son here could not be pardoned!"
    He ordered his underlings to grab him and administer
Forty heavy strokes to the emperor's father-in-law.
He also told two other people under his command
To shackle "that person named Cao" in iron shackles.
    He then gave orders to quickly go to the water-prison
And release Liu Sijun, who was held captive there.
When the young master saw the corpse of his wife,
He fell down and collapsed in the dust on the earth.
    "I urged you a hundred times, nay, a thousand times,
Not to go and sell your flowers out on the streets!
Today you have found your death on the streets,
So on whom can our three-year-old baby now rely?"
    When Judge Bao saw how bitterly he was weeping,
He had the corpse removed to the prefectural office.
The emperor's father-in-law knelt in the courtyard,
While Judge Bao took his seat in the hall above.
    Loudly he ordered that he be pulled down for a beating:
"Forty strokes with a heavy stick, show no mercy!
Chain his feet in shackles, lock his hands in a block,
And lock him up behind bars in the imperial prison."

Let's not sing of the emperor's father-in-law in prison,
But let's sing of the nine wives of the Cao mansion.
    These nine wives together sent a report to the Throne,
Reporting his imprisonment to His Majesty Renzong.
Once the Son of Heaven Renzong had seen the report,
He hastily issued an imperial edict, which left the court.
    And when this imperial edict entered the Kaifeng office,

It instructed Judge Bao of the Southern Office as follows:
"Whatever may have happened, please for my sake
Pardon my father-in-law, the person surnamed Cao."
   As soon as Judge Bao received the imperial edict,
He carefully read it from beginning to end, and
As soon as he finished reading, he flew into a rage,
Repeatedly cursing his lord as "a king without the Way."
   "Your father-in-law broke statutes and laws by the book,
And yet you issue an imperial edict to show him mercy!"

He returned the imperial edict to the golden palace hall,
And in his turn reported to His Imperial Majesty Renzong:
   "If you want to shield your father-in-law from justice,
You will have to appeal to King Yama for consideration,
Let alone this one imperial father-in-law surnamed Cao—
Even ten of his ilk would not be able to save their skins!"
   When his imperial edict was returned to the golden palace,
This completely enraged His Imperial Majesty Renzong.
   The empress hastily spoke up in the golden palace hall.
"I cannot just sit here in the palace; I will go there in person!
This old Bao has really become utterly insupportable.
I'll go to the Southern Office and save my father!"
   Once the emperor had agreed to her proposal,
Fierce palace women formed the empress's escort.
The empress mounted her jewel-studded sedan chair
And was followed by three hundred Hanlin troops.
   Eight hundred palace women to her left and right:
Eunuchs and palace ladies all followed along.
Leaving from the Chaoyang main palace courtyard,
She arrived at the prefectural office of Kaifeng City.

When Judge Bao heard of her arrival, he promptly
Performed the twenty-four bows due to her position.
   But as soon as the empress saw the face of Judge Bao,
She loudly cursed him for not being human.
"What feud ever did exist between you and the Caos
That you do your utmost to kill all those called Cao?

You were told to go to Chenzhou to distribute rice,
But you had to kill my elder brothers, both of them!
Killing my elder brothers should have been enough,
But today you want to go so far as to kill my father!

Hand my father over to me, as quickly as possible,
And all other matters I'll not pursue, I'll let them rest.
But if you stubbornly refuse to hand over my father,
I'll make sure you won't be an official any longer."

Once she had cursed Judge Bao with only one word,
He started to loudly curse Her Majesty the empress.
"It's your father who has broken the law by the book,
And yet you dare wildly curse me, this high official!

I have ruled in seventy-two cases of miscarriage of justice,
And in each of these cases I have given a fair ruling.
Taking into account that Your Majesty is the empress,
I'll have you given ten or twenty merciless strokes!"

He ordered two of his servants on his left and his right
To fetch that person surnamed Cao from his prison.
"His Majesty bestowed on me an imperial sword,
With which I may kill both my lord and his vassals.

When I have beheaded the imperial father-in-law,
I'll hang his head from the gate of the prefectural office."
A weeping empress, riding her jewel-studded sedan chair
And followed by her full retinue, returned to the palace.

As the next item of business Judge Bao ordered his servants
To pull the bronze nail out of the mouth of lady Zhang.
He ordered them to lift up her corpse and gently place it
On the bench used to call back the soul of the deceased.

The cushion and the girdle that bring back the soul—
Her three souls and seven spirits returned to this earth.

It was just as if this woman had been having a dream,
And when she opened her eyes, she looked all around.
When she lifted her head and saw her dear husband,
She rose from the bed and pulled him close to her.

Husband and wife, both of them, were awash in tears

And expressed their gratitude to Clear-Sky Judge Bao.
The two of them knelt down on the cinnabar floor and
Called out repeatedly, "Your Excellency Clear-Sky!"

He also ennobled the virtuous and filial lady Zhang,
Ennobling her as a Lady of the first rank of nobility.
When Sijun and his wife had received this honor,
They bowed toward the court to express their thanks.

They also bowed to Judge Bao of the Southern Office,
Bowing to thank him for the grace of saving their lives.
Judge Bao then answered them in the following words:
"You good woman, please listen to what I have to say.

You are a woman who practices virtue and filial piety.
I will report your name to His Majesty, the emperor,
So he will award rank and position to both of you,
And you may return home in glory, with high status!"

Judge Bao immediately ascended the golden palace hall
And presented his report to His Majesty, the emperor.

The empress, from her side, also had prepared a report;
She, too, submitted it to His Imperial Majesty Renzong.
"Your Majesty, please kill that couple, so you may
Remedy the injustice that has been done to my father!"

Once he heard this, Judge Bao was filled with rage,
And he loudly cursed the empress for not being human.
"Your father, while being the emperor's father-in-law,
Pressured common women to become his concubines!

He had this woman flower peddler beaten to death and
Had her buried in the flower garden on the western side.
If not for me, Wenzheng, of all those here in this court,
Where would the common people go to seek justice?

When breaking the law, prince and pauper are the same—
The laws of Xiao He do not allow us to show any mercy![10]
Yes, indeed, I'm proud to say I have killed your father,
So he may be reborn in his next existence as a better person.

The Jade Emperor in the sky has dispatched me to earth[11]
To help and assist His Sagely Majesty Renzong in his rule.
If it wasn't out of consideration for His Imperial Majesty,

I would make sure you were dethroned as empress!"
The Son of Heaven Renzong stepped down from his throne
And with both his hands assisted Judge Bao in rising up.
"My realm of rivers and mountains all depends on you,
So allow me to raise you to a higher rank here at court!"
Judge Bao knelt down again, calling out, "Your Majesty,
May Your Majesty be so kind as to listen to my words.
There's no need to give your servant some higher office,
But please award an office to this person surnamed Liu."
When His Majesty had heard this request from Judge Bao,
He appointed Liu Sijun to the official rank of a prefect.

After expressing his thanks, the latter returned to Antong,
Where friends and relatives, uncles and cousins all came,
With all their children, great and small, to welcome them—
Her own baby boy tugged at her gown, crying, "Mommy!"
The young lady grabbed the hand of her darling baby, and
Tears coursed down her cheeks, falling in ample profusion:
"Your mother had died, but she's been saved by Judge Bao,
So now the two of us, mother and son, are reunited again!"
She knelt down on her knees before the lady of the house,
And her mother-in-law, upon seeing her, was awash in tears.
The whole family, old and young, had now been reunited;
Bowing deeply, they expressed their thanks to Judge Bao.

As human beings we all should imitate young lady Zhang:
The fame of her virtue will be transmitted for all eternity!
All officials should take their example from Judge Bao, so
All wrongs of this world will be righted by their rulings!

10

THE DEMONIC CARP

Written out by Yi Nianhua

From the time when Pangu opened up heaven and earth,
The Three Emperors and the Five Thearchs settled the cosmos.[1]
The emperors Taizu and Taizong subdued the four borders;[2]
On all four borders their troops killed thousands of people.

The fifteenth of the Eighth Month is the festival of metal;[3]
A young girl got all dressed up and went out for a walk.
When this young girl came to a lake, she squatted down,[4]
And she looked at a fish that swam in the water.
    When it had drunk the girl's pure and bland water,[5]
It immediately changed itself into this girl's shape.
One change for the rouge, one change for the powder,
A third change, and the clothes were exactly the same!

This demonic carp was really brazen: butting and kicking
With head and feet, it knocked with its hand on the door.
As soon as the young man heard this resounding noise,
He promptly opened the door to see who might be there.
    "I am the young daughter of the Jins, of the Jin family;

I noticed how assiduously you are studying the books."
He opened wide the two wings of the gate of his study;
The young man invited this young girl to come inside.

When the girl had come inside and sat down on a chair,
The young man addressed her with the following words:
"What kind of business brings you here to my study?
Why did you come to my study in the middle of the night?"

"If you study by daytime, you'll obtain an official post,
But if you study at night, you will damage your spirit."

The young man answered her in the following words:
"Young lady, please listen to what I have to tell you:
If one studies at night, one will obtain an official post;
If you study by daytime, you'll be disturbed by others."

She sat there till the fifth watch, throughout the night,
Then the young girl got up and made ready to return.
The young man also got up in order to see her off;
He saw her out though the gate—she disappeared.

The young man turned back, closed the gate, and slept—
A hairpin of gold had been dropped near his study door.

He picked up the golden hairpin and took a good look;
It turned out to be a golden hairpin the young girl had lost.
The young man considered the matter carefully in his heart,
And then he asked his father and mother to have a look.

As soon as his parents saw the make of this golden hairpin,
They knew, "This is one of the engagements gifts we sent!"
His father and mother were greatly displeased in their hearts
And hastened to the Jin family to demand an explanation.

When they arrived at the Jin family and were let inside,
They berated the master of the house as a good-for-nothing.

"In view of the eminent official position you hold,
We feel we cannot but show you some consideration.
Buffaloes and horses are led back to the stable [at dusk],
But your daughter alone is not locked up for the night.

You may promise her to someone else; we don't want her:
For seven nights in a row she came to our son's study!

And in case you, dear sir, do not believe us, we have here
This golden hairpin, our engagement gift to her, as proof!"

When Sir Jin heard this, his heart was filled with rage;
He dispatched a servant girl to tell his daughter to come out.
"We have provided you with an embroidery room in which to sit;
You are not allowed to go outside the house at nighttime!"
    When the young girl heard this, she replied as follows:
"My dear daddy, please listen to what I have to say.
During daytime I keep my sister company all the time;
At night I sleep with my sister in one and the same bed.
    My brother's wife is also staying with us in the room;
Going down or coming up, the stairs squeak and creak.
I go outside only when I have to visit the toilet, and then
I am always accompanied by a couple of servant girls."
    "My daughter, I ask you again to tell me the truth:
How did you drop and lose this hairpin made of gold?
This golden hairpin originally came from his family.
I don't know which enemy wants to destroy us!"
    "I have stayed here at home in my embroidery room;
I have no idea where this enemy may come from.
Could it be, dear daddy, that you had thrown it out?
I lay my plaint before Judge Bao for his verdict!"

She ordered the family servants to get her a sedan chair,
And with her parents she went off to Kaifeng Prefecture.
Hurrying on, they quickly finished their entire journey
And arrived at the prefect's office in the city of Kaifeng.
    The written complaint was immediately submitted,
And when Judge Bao received it, he read it carefully.
"It appears that Sir Jin is the innocent victim of a crime,
And so implores me, Judge Bao, to give my verdict!"
    The young lady stepped forward and then knelt down.
"I beg you, Judge Bao, to clear my sullied name!
I am Sir Jin's daughter, raised in the inner chambers;
Of course I do not roam the streets during nighttime!

During daytime I'm my mother's constant companion;
If I leave her for a moment, it's only to wash my hands.
I stay in my embroidery room like any proper young lady;
It is impossible for me to go to someone's study at night!

    If I wanted to go out in order to have some fun—
There are two servant girls who follow me around!
This golden hairpin originally belonged to his family,
But I have no clue where my enemy is to be found."

Judge Bao, who was seated in the high hall of his office,
Got his precious mirror to pursue the truth of the matter.
His precious mirror revealed a demonic carp: that carp
Day after day went at night to the young man's study!

    That demonic carp sucked the young man's blood,
And the young man's face was chrysanthemum-yellow!
Judge Bao thereupon immediately went to the lake
And ordered his underlings to arrest this demonic carp.

    The demonic carp promptly changed its shape
And changed itself into a woman in a red vest.
But the precious mirror of Judge Bao revealed
The person in a red vest to be the demonic carp!

"How grateful we are to Judge Bao and his mirror;
Without Judge Bao this matter could not have been solved."
The young lady came forward and expressed her thanks;
She expressed her thanks to Judge Bao for his actions.

    "If I could not have relied on Your Honor, Judge Bao,
How would I have been able to clear my sullied name?
I am grateful to you, Judge Bao, for your clear verdict,
And all my life I will never dare forget your great grace."

If in this world we did not have His Honor, Judge Bao,
How could the common people's wrongs ever be cleared?

11

THE KARMIC AFFINITY OF LIANG SHANBO AND ZHU YINGTAI

Written out by Gao Yinxian

I will not sing of any former kings or of the Later Han;[1]
Listen as I sing the story of the charming girl Yingtai.
    Squire Zhu of Emei headed a very wealthy household;
The family was very wealthy, owning fields and farms.
His only child was a girl, who was very bright and smart,
And when she turned fifteen, she was quite a sight.
    She had no elder brother, she had no younger brother:
This one girl Yingtai was her father's only child!
Yingtai expressed the desire to go to Hangzhou;
She wanted to go to Hangzhou to enter the academy.
    This upset squire Zhu so much that he cursed her loudly:
"My daughter, what you're saying makes no sense!
    Only boys, you know, are allowed to enter an academy—
Have women ever been allowed to enter an academy?
If you insist on going to Hangzhou, I will have you
Hacked in two and thrown into the Yangzi River!"

The daughter answered her father as follows:
"My father, please listen to what I have to say!
    The bodhisattva Guanyin was originally a woman,

But she recited the sutras in the Buddha-hall all day.[2]
The Son of Heaven Zetian was born a woman,
But she managed the empire with true authority.[3]

Now squire Zhu of Emei is the father of a daughter
Who wants to go to Hangzhou and enter an academy.
A good girl can fight her way through a thousand troops;
A good horse can gallop into a myriad-man battle!"

Hearing these words, squire Zhu laughed heartily:
"My dear daughter, you are making quite a claim!

On your head you wear a tiny lotus-seed chaplet;
Your feet are shod in pearly slippers—a pair of boots!
Walk out through the gate and take a step, to see whether
You really resemble a manly officer of the court."[4]

In her right hand she carried a cooling parasol;
With her left hand she lifted a fine box of books.
She took her leave of her parents, set out on the journey;
As if carried by clouds, she escaped the inner apartments.

She crossed quite a number of mountains and ridges;
She crossed quite a number of rivers and streams.
When she had traveled quite a distance on her road,
She rested below pine trees to enjoy the cool breeze.

After she had been sitting there for just a while,
The wind blew through the trees, clinking and tinkling.
After her, a young student arrived, who with his
Dragon gait and tiger steps was someone quite special!

Yingtai rose to her feet and greeted him with a bow;
In a soft voice, whispering, she asked the question,
"May I ask you, my brother, where are you going?"
And he, too, wanted to ask where Yingtai was going.

Yingtai answered the student in the following words:
"Sir, please listen to the words I have to say.

I am a son of the Zhu family of this prefecture;
My name is Yingtai; I have one older sibling.[5]
And because there is no academy in this region,
I want to go to Hangzhou to enter the academy."

The student answered Yingtai in the following way:

"Yingtai, please listen to what I have to say in my turn.
I am a son of the Liang family of this prefecture;
My name is Shanbo; I am the eldest of my siblings.
And because there is no academy in our region,
I, too, am on my way to Hangzhou for the academy!"
  The two of them decided to become sworn brothers
Who would deliberate together about all problems.
The eldest in years would act as the elder brother;
The youngest in years would act as the younger brother.
  The elder brother, eldest in years, walked in front;
The younger brother, youngest in years, carried the books.
In this way they eventually arrived in Hangzhou;
From afar they saw Hangzhou's fine academy!

Each and every one says that Hangzhou is beautiful;
That fame is not falsely spread throughout the world.
Not only does the upper street have lamb and pork for sale;
The lower street perfumes the city with flowers and wine.
  On the street they bought a sheet of fine cotton paper;
With this letter they visited the Kong mansion school.
They first bowed before the teacher as their father;
Next they bowed before the teacher as their parent.[6]
  Thirdly they bowed before his three thousand disciples;
Bowing deeply, they honored them on entering the school.
Fourthly they bowed to the Sage, and when that was done,
'Twas brushes and inkstone, and books and their chests.
  During daytime they walked together and sat together;
At nighttime they shared one blanket and one couch.

During nighttime Yingtai slept with all her clothes on;
She did not take off her clothes when she went to bed.
From this behavior Shanbo immediately figured out,
Immediately figured out that Yingtai had to be a girl.
  "You must be a girl, because otherwise why would you
Refuse to take off your clothes before going to bed?
Tonight you also should take off your clothes—
There is no harm in sleeping without one's clothes!"

Yingtai answered Shanbo in the following words:
"Dear brother, please listen to what I have to say.

My parents back home are experts in sewing clothes,
And they made these clothes for me to fit my body.
These clothes are fitted with twenty-four loops,
And correspondingly there are two dozen buttons.

Putting these clothes on takes from dusk till midnight;
Taking these clothes off takes from midnight till dawn.
It would take me from morning till night, without end,
But when I rise tomorrow, I have to recite my texts.

If you now insist that I sleep without clothes,
Put four cups of water on all four sides of the bed.
And if one drop of water is spilled by your moving,
You will accept forty strokes of the bamboo ruler!"

All students at the school will join in the beating—
Even if you weren't going to be beaten, you'd still be scared!
A frightened Shanbo was filled with fear and didn't dare
Turn around even once until the arrival of dawn.

He slept till midnight and then stepped outside to pee,
But Yingtai squatted down by the side of the bed,
And she answered his question in the following way:
"Dear brother, please listen to what I have to say.

People who study books revere Heaven and Earth:
Above us are the sun and moon and also the stars.
During daytime there are divine immortals passing by;
During nighttime the Dipper illuminates the world.[7]

To urinate while standing up is the way of beasts;
To lower one's body to defecate is the way of gods."

When Yingtai combed her hair and washed her face,
She took a piece of soap and rubbed her bosom.
In so doing, she displayed a pair of fragrant nipples,
And both her breasts were as white as snow.

Yingtai answered Shanbo's question as follows:
"Dear brother, please listen to what I have to say.
People who have good luck have large breasts,

But people without good luck have no breasts.
A man with large breasts will achieve high office,
But a girl with large breasts will lead a lonely life."
In this way she fooled her brother Shanbo utterly;
She managed to fool him promptly time and again.

But the middle of the Seventh Month arrived again,
The date to go to the rear courtyard and take a bath.
Five hundred students went there to take baths;
Each of them took a bath before returning home.
The only one not to take a bath was Yingtai;
At that time she was so upset she turned yellow
Because all the students of the school figured out,
Immediately figured out that Yingtai was a girl.
Yingtai answered them all in the following way:
"Fellow students, please listen to what I have to say.
I have no desire whatsoever now to take a bath;
I'll wrap up my study of the books and go home.
I'm afraid that my parents are getting on in years,
And I also left my unmarried sister behind.
Cow and horse return for the night to their shed—
Can a human being not long to return home?"

Yingtai had studied the books for a full three years;
In her heart she had memorized a bellyful of texts.
Shanbo had studied the books for a full three years;
His fine skills at government were without compare.
Yingtai then secretly thought to herself,
"I should return home and serve my parents!
If one does not exhaust oneself in filial caring,
One cannot be counted a human being and filial son."
After she had taken her leave of Master Kong,
She took her leave of her teacher and fellow students.
Once she had taken her leave of her fellow students,
She also took her leave of elder brother Liang Shanbo.
The latter gathered his things and accompanied her,
And on the road she spoke her mind time and again.

"Elder brother, you've accompanied me to this wall;
Above it I see a fine branch of a pomegranate tree.
I would like to pick a pomegranate for you, my brother,
But fear you'd find it so tasty you'd want to steal one."[8]

"Elder brother, you've accompanied me to this pond.
Looking down in the pond, we see our reflected faces.
With the karma, people will meet despite a thousand miles;
Without the karma, even neighbors will not get together."

"Elder brother, you have accompanied me to this well;
On the water of this well is a pair of mandarin ducks.
One of them is a drake, and the other is a female duck;
The only party lacking here is the matchmaker."

"Elder brother, you have accompanied me to the river;
On the riverbank is the boat of a fisherman.
Only the boat will go and moor at the bank,
But the bank will never go and moor at the boat."

When they walked to the wharf to be ferried across,
The ferryman refused to take them for lack of money.
With all her clothes on Yingtai jumped into the water,
And from the water she said the following few lines,
    "Water soaks the Dragon Gate: the character *ding* and *kou*;
Soon it will soak through to the side of the character *ke*.[9]
    Elder brother, if you can find the solution to that,
I'll discuss the matter again with you farther on.
But, elder brother, if you cannot solve this riddle,
You return to the academy while I return home."
    Shanbo answered Yingtai in the following manner:
"Now please listen to what I have to say.
You may want to leave, but I will not leave yet;
I'll return to the academy while you return home."
    Yingtai answered Shanbo in the following way:
"Let me ask you everything, from the beginning.
    Having studied for three years, you know morals,

So why do you not turn around and go home?
But in case you ever come and look for me,
Make sure to come inside and have a cup of tea.
    Following Five-Miles Arch is Seven-Flower Ridge;
No wind for ten miles, yet you smell the flowers.
If it storms at night, there's snow on the mountains;
All kinds of fowl and geese and ducks fill the pond.
    That place is the place where your Yingtai lives,
At the foot of Mount Emei, in Zhu Family Village."

Let's not sing of how Yingtai traveled back home;
Let's sing of Shanbo, who returned to the academy.
    From the moment Shanbo saw that Yingtai had left,
His heart was filled with sorrow, filled with gloom.
When he thought back on the words she had spoken,
Each and every word was a riddle he could not solve.
    Confronted with statements, a gentleman ponders and asks;
He will have no peace until he achieves clear understanding.
So he asked a fortune-teller to draw a hexagram,
And the diviner's hexagram was very lucky indeed:
    "Firstly, I find that your beloved is not far from here;
Secondly, I find that marriage is quite fitting right now.
Dear sir, start out today, and return to your family—
There is no need for further study, quickly go home!"
    When Shanbo now heard him talk in this manner,
He ran, as if carried on clouds, back to his school.

He took his leave of his teacher and his benefactor,
Turned around on his feet—off to Zhu Family Village!
When he espied the gate, he saw a fine mansion:
The roof of glazed tiles offered a beautiful sight.
    Shanbo promptly asked the little boy at the gate:
"I am looking for Second Son Zhu of the academy.
We studied together at the master's court in Hangzhou;
For three years we shared the same blanket and couch."
    The young boy answered Shanbo as follows:
"Dear sir, please listen to what I have to say.

Here we have only Second Sister Zhu who studies;
We've never seen a Second Son Zhu who studies.
   She is a pretty girl of a quite different family,
So how could she have shared your blanket and couch?
It's a good thing squire Zhu hasn't heard this—
If the old man had heard this, you'd be locked out."

When her servant girl heard this, she ran off to report,
To report his arrival to Zhu Yingtai in her room:
   "Outside at the gate a young man has arrived who
Was asking for a Second Son Zhu of the academy.
They were together at the master's court in Hangzhou;
For three years he shared the same couch with him."
   When Yingtai heard this, she quickly put on her clothes,
A woman dressed in male disguise—quite extraordinary!
She came to the gate in order to ask him inside and
Hastily ordered the servant girl to brew them some tea.
   She ordered the servants to set out a banquet with wine,
And the two of them sat opposite each other, talking texts.
When squire Zhu came by to observe the situation,
He promptly called Yingtai over and questioned her:
   "Which prefecture does this guy come from? Which county?
What is his surname and name? And where does he live?
What kind of business brings him to our family, and why
Are you and he comparing examination essays?"
   Yingtai answered her father in the following manner:
"My dear father, please listen to what I have to say.
   He is a son of the Liang family of this very prefecture;
His bellyful of fine talent is without equal in this world.
We were together at the master's court in Hangzhou;
For three years we shared our blanket and books."
   Hearing these words, squire Zhu was filled with joy;
He treated the young man in the warmest way, was greatly concerned.
Considering their deep friendship at the academy, he had
A horse saddled in order to take him quickly back home.
   Yingtai then spoke to Shanbo the following words:
"Please do not waste your mind in thirsting for me—

If in this life we cannot be united in marriage, we will
Be a couple in each following life, each new existence!"

As soon as Shanbo turned around, he became ill.
Filled with love-longing all the way, he came home.
When his mother had not yet seen him coming back,
She had been busily burning incense right in the road.
    "Originally you said you'd go and study for three years.
Why haven't you returned after all this time?"
She had not yet finished these words, when he arrived!
His mother immediately said to Shanbo the following words:
    "When you left, your face was as pink as peach blossoms;
Now you return, your face as yellow as chrysanthemums.
It must be that you rose too early and suffered the dew;
It must be that at night you conducted some hidden affair."
    Shanbo answered his mother in the following way:
"My dear mother, please listen to my explanation.
    It is not that I rose too early and suffered the dew;
It is not that at night I conducted some hidden affair.
When three years ago I left home and set out,
I happened to meet Second Son Zhu on the road.
    'So you are the son of the Zhu family of Emei,
Also on your way to Hangzhou to enter the academy!'
Together we were in the master's court in Hangzhou;
For three years we shared our blanket and books.
    When he left, he still was a regular guy, but then
When I came back, he had turned into a pretty girl!
When I saw how smart and intelligent she was,
I was overcome with longing to become a couple!"
    The mother answered the son in the following way:
"I myself will act as the matchmaker on your behalf!"

She went to the Zhu mansion and sat down in the hall.
When squire Zhu came in, she spoke as follows:
"Many thanks for your help to my son yesterday night.
It was very kind of you to help him travel back home.
    On the road he contracted the illness of love-longing,

Which at night especially brings truly unbearable pain.
The only way for my son to recover from this disease
Is for him to be married and become a couple with your daughter."
 Squire Zhu answered her in the following manner:
"My dear lady, please listen to my words. If only you
Had arrived three days earlier, I'd have happily agreed,
But now I've already promised her to young Mr. Ma."

When Yingtai in her room heard what had been discussed,
She hastily dressed herself in her finest shift and skirt.
 She wore brilliant hairpins of pearls and kingfisher feathers,
Her feet shod in wood-soled shoes with phoenix-tips.
With her willow-leaf brows and peach-blossom cheeks
She resembled an immortal maiden descending to earth.
 Yingtai came from her room to sit with Liang's mother,
And she ordered her servant girl to brew some nice tea.
Liang's mother spoke to Yingtai in the following way:
"Dear Miss Zhu, please listen to what I have to say.
 Yesterday night my son came by and imposed on you;
Now today he is tied to his bed by a wasting illness.
The only way for my son to recover from this disease
Is for him to be married to you, so that you form a couple."
 Yingtai then answered the old lady as follows:
"My dear lady, please listen to what I have to say.
 While I was in Hangzhou to study the books,
My father went ahead and found me a marriage partner.
He accepted the rich engagement gifts of the Ma family,
The engagement gifts of a goose, and a goat, and a pig.
 Be so kind as to take this message to brother Shanbo:
Please do not waste your mind in thirsting for me—
In this life we may not succeed in being husband and wife;
After our deaths, at the Yellow Springs, we'll be a couple!"[10]

"If you want elder brother to recover from his illness,
I will write on your behalf a most miraculous recipe.
Firstly you need the eastern ocean's dragon king's horn,
Secondly, the western mountains' phoenix king's crest;

Thirdly you need the horn on the head of a unicorn;
Fourthly you need the congee on a white dove's back;
Fifthly you need the gall of a cat, a thousand years old,
Sixthly the frost on top of tiles ten thousand years old;
 Seventhly water from the Jade Emperor's pure vase,
Eighthly the Queen Mother of the West's longevity peaches;
Ninthly you need a golden lad to simmer the medicine,
And tenthly you need a jade maiden to serve the potion.[11]
 If you cannot obtain these ten miraculous ingredients,
My elder brother's soul will go and meet with King Yama.[12]
 In the unfortunate event of brother Liang's passing away,
Make sure to bury him by the side of the Ma family road.
Erect for him a stele of blue stone and inscribe in the middle
Of that stele the name of brother Liang, Liang Shanbo!
 One day his sworn sister will pass by his grave and offer
A sacrifice of the three animals and a libation of wine,
Hoping with all her heart to be received by brother Liang!"[13]
 His mother was overcome by sadness because of her words;
She went home and gave a full report to her son Shanbo.
When Shanbo heard the marriage proposal had been rejected,
His depression turned into an illness that carried him away.

But let's not sing of Shanbo and the way he passed away;
Let's sing once again of the new groom of the Ma family!
When Yingtai had stepped into the colorful sedan chair,
She inquired of her escort while on the road, asking,
 "My sworn brother of my Hangzhou days, Liang Shanbo—
Where was he buried? Would someone be able to tell me?"
When they had looked around, they came back and told her,
"This grave just happens to be the one of Liang Shanbo!"
 Yingtai left her sedan chair, weeping heartrendingly,
And as she did so, she cried out, "Dear brother Liang!
If your spirit has the power, please open this grave,
So we may be a couple on the Yellow Springs road!"
 Before she had finished her words, the grave mound
Opened with a booming sound, split in the middle!
Yingtai rushed forward and jumped into the grave—

All those who watched it were overcome by panic!
　　Her phoenix-shoes and gauze skirt—all torn to pieces!
That very moment that pretty girl disappeared!
When the Ma family rushed forward to open the grave,
The lovers flew up to heaven, changed into mandarin ducks.

Shanbo had been a golden lad who descended to earth,
Yingtai a jade maiden who came down to mortal dust.
The two of them together went off to the heavenly palace,
Where they then paid their respects to the Jade Emperor.
　　This is the end of the story of Yingtai and Shanbo—
Leave it to later generations as their reading matter.

12

FIFTH DAUGHTER WANG

Transcribed by Hu Cizhu

I will not tell of the Han, and I will not tell of the Tang;[1]
I will sing of Fifth Daughter Wang who read the sutras.
Like one drop of the Three Pearls, transmitted to earth—
The Twenty-four Exemplars of Filial Piety: such was her virtue![2]

 If you want to know where Fifth Daughter was from,
Listen to all the facts of her case from the very beginning.
She hailed from Nanhui County in Caozhou Prefecture,
From Zhao Family Village in the township of Qingping.

 Her father sir Wang Shou had sired this one daughter,
Had sired this one daughter who excelled above all others.
In the sequence of sisters she was Fifth Daughter Wang,
And the name that had been chosen for her was Jixiang.

 At the ages of one and two she was very smart indeed;
At the ages of three and four she did not leave the room.
She did not drink water from a pond for raising fish
And no boiled water heated for slaughtering animals.

 From the ages of seven to fifteen she read the sutras, and
At the age of nineteen she was promised to the Zhaos.
But each day she burned three or five sticks of incense

And, seated in lotus position, recited the Diamond Sutra.
She recited the sutra from early in the morning till noon;
She then recited the sutra from dusk till break of dawn.
Her father and mother were very much displeased, as
They wanted to marry their daughter off to her husband-to-be.

They married her to Lingfang to be husband and wife:
They walked together and sat together as mandarin ducks,
And by the time they had been a couple for only three years,
She had given birth to both a baby boy and a baby girl.
For the boy the name that was selected was Xiaoyu;
For the girl the name that was selected was Xinxiang.

Her husband Lingfang was not given to pious practice;
With two pointed knives he butchered pigs and goats.
Each day he butchered no less than three or five pigs,
Ordering his wife lady Wang to heat the scalding water.

As lady Wang was heating the water, awash in tears,
She kindly admonished her husband Zhao Lingfang
To choose some other profession and do good deeds,
Not to spend his life on earth slaughtering animals.

"A white knife goes in, and then a red knife comes out;
Even if one doesn't want to shiver, one still will shiver!
This killing of living animals accumulates many sins;
In the underworld you will be unable to cross the river.

If you stop this killing of animals, don't do it anymore,
You will be liberated in a next life and rise to heaven."

Lingfang answered lady Wang in the following words:
"What you are saying there is not at all well considered.
You recite your Diamond Sutra and accumulate your blessings,
And I'll butcher my goats and pigs and suffer for my sins.

You people given to pious practice, don't bother me;
Don't come in here and bore me with all your tall tales.
All the many things you need from early morning onward,
Salt and oil and wood and rice—on whom do you rely?

The clothes you wear, the rice you eat—who pays for that?
My family has been butchers now for nine generations.

Don't tell me that this profession has no good side:
From this bowl of blood we buy our fields and farms!

　　Practice evil, and you don't see an evil retribution;
Do good deeds, and you will not be fortunate forever.
Butcher Zhang slaughtered pigs and became an immortal,
But Li Si read the sutras and died far before his time.[3]

　　This killing of living animals is only a minor matter;
An addiction to gambling is the worst sin in a man.

　　By applying cosmetics, you commit far greater sins,
By sticking flowers in your hair, insupportable crimes.
And how many pairs of silk shoes do you wear out
In the three hundred sixty days of one single year?[4]

　　In giving birth to boy or girl, you commit many sins:
Those many bowls of soiled water and washing water!

　　If you throw the water down the inside covered drain,
You pollute the virgin lads of our house and garden.[5]
If you throw the water into the field sown with grain,
You pollute the Three Lights: sun, moon, and stars.
And if you throw the water below the feet of the bed,
You pollute the god of the soil, rob him of his ease.

　　If you walk past the hearth before the third day,[6]
You pollute the fire of the hearth, the god of the stove.
If you walk through the hall before the fifth day,
You pollute the gods and immortals inside the house.

　　If you walk past the sutra-chapel before the seventh day,
You pollute the incense burner in front of the Buddha.
And if you fetch water from the river that first month,
You pollute the dragon kings in all oceans and lakes."

When lady Wang heard him lecture in this manner,
She could not stop herself from bursting out crying.
"If I also commit sins by giving birth to a boy or a girl,
I should have stayed at home as an unmarried daughter!

　　As long as you didn't tell me, things were still fine,
But now I've heard you tell all this, my heart is pained.
If doing that kind of thing comes with so many sins,

We may still share one house—but in separate beds!"
    When Lingfang heard her speak these words, [he said,]
"My dear wife, what you say is not well considered!
'Husband and wife' lasts as long as heaven and earth;
You're breaking apart a couple of mandarin ducks.
    If today you do insist on sleeping in separate beds,
You'll have to answer these questions about the Diamond Sutra:
How many characters are there in the Diamond?
How many chapters are there? How many 'diamonds'?
    Which word is the opening word, which the concluding?
And which word is the word that comes in the middle?
If you, my dear wife, know the answer to these questions,
I will no longer object to sleeping in separate beds."
    Lady Wang answered her husband in the following way:
"My dear husband, please listen to what I have to say.
    The Diamond counts five thousand four hundred words;
There are thirty-two chapters, and then eight 'diamonds.'
The opening word is 'thus,' the final one is 'recite,' and
The two words 'what means' come right in the middle."
    When Lingfang heard lady Wang speak in this manner,
Not a single word was wrong, not even half a sentence!

Husband and wife, the two of them, led separate lives,
Each in a separate room, sleeping on a separate bed.
She did not apply cosmetics, did not wear any flowers,
And in doing her hair, used only water to make it shine.
    With black soap and heated water she washed her body;
She washed and cleansed her body, put on other clothes:
On her head she wore only a kerchief to wrap her hair,
And her feet she now shod in a pair of straw sandals.
    Her body was dressed in a gown and a cap of the Way,
And a chaplet of pearls always hung before her breast.
By day and by night she recited the sutra without rest,
Beating out the rhythm on the resounding wooden fish.[7]
    When walking, she resembled Shuyu, so very proper;[8]
When seated, she looked like Guanyin descending to hell.

Her heart was not intent on separating from her husband;
Her heart was intent only on reciting the Diamond Sutra.

The eighteen arhats were arranged to the left and right;
Also the gods of the soil had been placed on both sides.
In the center was found a threesome of Tathagata Buddhas:
These she revered in her Buddha-hall day in, day out!

As she recited the words of the Diamond Sutra so well,
She started to scare the ten judges of the world of shade.[9]
When King Yama heard her recite the Diamond Sutra,
He called over his ox-headed and horse-faced demons.

"I now order you to go to the world of light, to go and
Check on the lads of good and evil in the world of light:
Those who are good will live, the evil will be punished,
And all unfilial sons will be locked up in the cowshed."

Hearing this order, the ox-headed and horse-faced demons
Went to the world of light to investigate conditions there.
They investigated from the eastern border to the western regions:
Southward they went up to the temple halls of Mount Emei;

Westward they went up to the Buddha's Western Paradise;
Northward they went up to Yangzhou's ghost-killing field.
They visited all prefectures and counties of the empire,
But even so they failed to locate even one unfilial son.

But when they came to the county of Nanhui in Caozhou,
To Zhao Family Village in the township of Qingping,
They found there lady Wang, who was reading the sutras—
The husband she was married to was Zhao Lingfang.

This woman had accumulated good deeds since birth,
As she spent her life reciting the sutras day and night.

When the ox-headed and horse-faced demons passed
Her house, they didn't dare loudly ask their questions:
Three flames emerged from the head of this woman,
Flames of fire that brightly lit the sutra-chapel.

The ox-headed and horse-faced demons didn't dare
Arrest her and hastened back to report to King Yama:
"Throughout the world of light there's not one evil son;

There's only that good person, Fifth Daughter Wang!
It's all because she recites the sutras in the Buddha-hall—
Five-colored auspicious clouds light up the sutra-chapel.
Because she can recite the Diamond Sutra to perfection,
We, minor ghosts, didn't dare enter her Buddha-hall!"

When King Yama heard them speak in this manner, he
Promptly wanted to question her on the Diamond Sutra.
He dispatched one pair of virgin lads clad in black, and
He also dispatched one pair of virgin lads clad in white,
To go and arrest that lady Wang in the world of light, to
Be questioned on the Diamond Sutra in the underworld.
"Don't lose any time in talking; be gone and make haste!
Go quickly and return quickly, so she may be interrogated!
For this mission you'll have a time limit of three full hours;
If you are late, I will have you beheaded, as sure as hell!"
Having received this order, the virgin lads wasted no time;
Crossing the border line, they arrived in the world of light
And went to the county of Nanhui in Caozhou Prefecture,
Then to Zhao Family Village in the township of Qingping.
Fifth Daughter Wang, who recited the sutras every day—
As she did so in the Buddha-hall, her face emitted a light.
When the virgin lads approached the sutra-chapel, they heard
The rhythm beaten out on the resounding wooden fish.
The four virgin lads were at a loss, as they did not know
By which way they might manage to enter the sutra-chapel.
In their desperation the virgin lads came up with a plan
And took on the guise of students on their way to school.
As soon as lady Wang saw them, she immediately asked,
"What brings you all to this sutra-chapel?
From which prefecture and which county do you hail?
Which village are you from? And from which township?
Whatever business you may have, I wouldn't know a thing;
In case you have any business, ask my husband, Mr. Zhao.
Reciting the sutras, I don't concern myself with other matters;
With all my heart I am devoted to reciting my Diamond!"

The four virgin lads couldn't stop themselves from laughing,
From laughing at this Fifth Daughter Wang and her sutras.

"Because of your reciting this sutra in the world of light,
You have even scared King Yama in the world of shade.
King Yama has dispatched us to come here and fetch you,
So you may answer his questions about the Diamond Sutra."

As soon as lady Wang had heard these words from the lads,
She could not stop herself from bursting into tears, saying,

"All I do is recite my sutra here in this world of mortals,
So how could I scare King Yama into taking such action?
Let him wait till my son and daughter are fully grown up;
It's no problem at all if you come and fetch me that time.

I will give you some gold and silver to go on your way;
Please arrest someone else whom you may present to King Yama.
Arrest someone with the same name and same surname;
Say that she is the Fifth Daughter Wang who reads sutras!"

The virgin lads answered lady Wang in the following way:
"Dear woman who reads sutras, please listen to our words:

It would be no problem to go and arrest someone else, but
Who'd be able to recite the sutra and answer the questions?
You may have gold and silver aplenty, but these are of no use;
When the underworld's warrant arrives, no god can help!

King Yama doesn't care for age when he makes an arrest;
Even three-year-old babies have to make the journey.
Since the beginning of time, one who is born also must die,
And even a hundred years cannot change the day of death."

When lady Wang heard this, she [said], awash in tears,
"You four virgin lads, please listen to what I have to say:

As you arrest me to appear before the underworld court,
I will let go of this life and make that journey with you.
Now you, virgin lads, each hold your merciless sword,
And I will follow you as you walk on both sides of me."

Lady Wang burned paper money and one stick of incense
And once again with great care recited the Diamond Sutra.
After saying good-bye to the threesome of Tathagata Buddhas,

She took her leave of the King of the Stove in the kitchen.
"Master of Fate, you are actually the master of the house,
On each last day of the month you ascend to High Heaven.[10]

Please relate many good words to the Jade Emperor, and
Please do not report on any evil deed to Highest Heaven.
I am now set to die and to return to the realm of shade,
So I won't come to the kitchen anymore to make tea."

She took three slivers of fragrant eaglewood from her chest,
Heated the water herself, then took a bath to wash her body.
Having cleansed her body, she said good-bye to the ancestors
And also to the brothers of her husband and their wives.

"We lived in the same house for a full thirteen years,
And never an evil word was spoken between all of us.

I leave behind a son and a daughter who are still very young,
So I hope that you, their uncles, will take good care of them.
If my daughter and son grow up and reach adulthood,
They will gloriously continue the ancestral sacrifices."

After she had said good-bye to the brothers of her husband,
She brought out another woman's chest from her own room.
Having retrieved from that chest a copy of the Diamond Sutra,
She buried it in the kitchen, next to the stove, [and said,]

"If it is fated that my husband and I will be reunited,
I will retrieve this Diamond Sutra, and we will be a couple."

After she was done burying this copy of the Diamond Sutra,
She turned around and went in one step to the sutra-chapel.
There she took a goat-hair brush, and using this brush,
She wrote three columns of characters on her left leg.

Lady Wang then came to the main hall of the house; there
She addressed her husband as follows: "Dear Zhao Lingfang,

By my recitation of the sutras here in the Buddha-hall,
I have scared the ten judges of the underworld courts.
Now King Yama has sent his agents to come and take me
To his realm to answer questions on the Diamond Sutra.

I had hoped that husband and wife would grow old together,
But who could have known that today I would die first?

I am only thirty-two years old, and yet we are separated!
So you, my husband, are bound to marry a second wife.

Both my infant son and infant daughter I entrust to you—
An infant son and an infant daughter, two different minds!
First there is this boy, and then there is also this girl—
On whom can this boy and girl rely without their mother?"

When Lingfang heard his wife speak in this manner,
He was dumbstruck and kept silent, at a loss for what to do.

"Husband and wife originally are birds sharing a grove—
But during drought and famine, each has to fend for itself.
If in this life we cannot stay a couple as husband and wife,
We must have burned short incense in an earlier existence."

Once she was done saying good-bye to her husband,
She also said good-bye to her darling son and daughter:

"I had hoped that mother and son would live forever,[11]
But who would have known that today I would die first?
When you, my darling son and daughter, have grown up,
Remember me who gave you birth and sweep my grave.

Now I pass from this world and leave you two behind;
Your father is bound to find himself a second wife, and
When he has found a second wife, serve her most filially,
Because a stepmother is quite unlike your own mother!

If your own mother beats you, she cries as much as you,
But when your stepmother beats you, she'll draw blood!
In sweeping the house, first sweep your stepmother's room,
And make sure no dust flies into your stepmother's room.

If she tells you to go to the east, you run toward the east;
If she tells you to go to the west, you run toward the west.

And never complain about your stepmother to your father,
Because if you do, your father will curse your stepmother,
And if he curses your stepmother, she'll take it out on you—
At the end of the day it is still you who are bound to suffer.

When a cloud hides the sun, a shadow crosses the hills—
The second wife of the first husband is still your mother."

She then gave her darling son the breast for some milk:

"This mother's milk is the last that I will let you drink!
I leave behind my son and daughter, both still so young—
How pitiable are my son and daughter without a mother!"

The mother and her two children were separated, torn apart!
She also said good-bye to her chest with its gilding of gold.
    She said good-bye to her bed and to the cushion on the bed:
"I'll not again mount the bed to receive the phoenix crown."
She said good-bye to the clothes racks in her room:
"I will never again take shift or gown from these racks."
    After she had said good-bye to all the objects in her room,
She said good-bye to the ancestral tablets in their shrine.
    "The name I'm known by is as a daughter of the Wangs;
I will never again exchange the water or burn incense.
I have buried one copy of the sutra in the room with the stove,
And so I have damaged a section of the wall in the kitchen."
    That very moment lady Wang collapsed on the floor,
As she hastily hurried forward to call on King Yama.
The virgin lads clad in black chained her with shackles;
The virgin lads clad in white followed behind her.

When Lingfang saw his wife tumbling down on the floor,
He loudly wailed three times: "Dear Fifth Daughter Wang!"
Her son and daughter wept and wailed their hearts out, and
Her brothers- and sisters-in-law also came over to weep.
    Close and distant relatives all donned mourning clothes:
As far as the eye could see, everyone dressed in white!
They hired an exorcist to open the road [for the coffin];
They also invited Buddhist monks to perform the rites.
    And when on the seventh day the rites were finished,
They lifted her up and carried lady Wang to her grave.
Pine and cypress were planted on the sides of the grave
To protect it against the clouds and the frost.

Now the matter of the funeral has been fully finished;
I'll sing again of lady Wang who had left this world.

The virgin lads informed lady Wang in these words:
"Dear woman who reads the sutras, please listen to us.
In the world of light your road has the sun and moon;
In the underworld there's nothing to light your road.

After we cross the border sign for the world of shade,
We will arrive, pressing on, at the Hill of Slippery Oil.
For every three steps forward, you slide four steps back:
The hardships presented by this hill are insupportable!"

Lady Wang promptly asked them the following question:
"Why is it called by the name 'Hill of Slippery Oil'?"
The virgin lads answered lady Wang in the following way:
"Dear woman, please listen to what we have to say.

Those who practiced good deeds all pass with no problem,
But those who did evil deeds all are thrown down this hill.
On the first and fifteenth one should observe the fast;
By drinking lots of monthly . . ., one avoids disaster.[12]

It is because mortal people do not observe the taboos;
By baking in oil and simmering over a fire, they sin.
Your account in the world of light is kept here below;
Breaking the [laws and] precepts are not minor sins.

It's up to you to practice evil in the world of light,
But here below you can't cross the Hill of Slippery Oil."

When they [easily] had passed this Hill of Slippery Oil,
They arrived, pressing on, at the Hill of Wasted Money.[13]
"In the world of light, incense and paper money are burned
On the first day of the four seasons and the eight sections.

When burning money, one should not grab a bundle;
By grabbing and tearing, the money doesn't make bills.
When later you want to take it out, no one will take it—
That money was used for this Hill of Wasted Money."

When they had passed by the Hill of Wasted Money,
They arrived at a terrace, called "Looking Back Home."

When she ascended the terrace and looked around,
She saw far away her dear husband Zhao Lingfang.

She also saw her son and her daughter back at home;
The whole family, old and young, was awash in tears.
    When lady Wang saw this, she secretly was thinking;
She secretly was thinking she wanted to go back home.
    But the virgin lads promptly advised her as follows:
"Dear woman who reads the sutras, please listen to us.
If we allowed you to return to the world of light,
Who will answer the questions about the Diamond Sutra?"

When they had passed the Looking Back Home terrace,
They arrived, pressing on, at the First-rate Teahouse.
A granny of eighty was operating a teahouse there;
Golden lads and jade maidens were serving the tea.
    Lady Wang had grown thirsty because of the walking,
So she wanted to go inside and drink some of this tea.
The four virgin lads addressed her, speaking as follows:
"Dear lady Wang, please listen to what we have to say.
    This place is not your ordinary common teahouse;
They serve the underworld's soul-confusing brew:
Once you've drunk this brew, nothing serious happens,
But you'll forget all the events of your lifetime.
    King Yama wants to question you about your sutra:
How would you be able to answer him about the Diamond?"
When lady Wang heard them give this explanation,
She decided to suffer her thirst and not drink the tea.

When they had passed this pavilion where tea was sold,
They suddenly arrived at the Pass of Ghost Gate.
The commander of ghosts on the west raised his club,
Ready to hit that lady Wang who reads the sutras.
    The virgin lads promptly addressed him as follows:
"Commander of ghosts, please listen to our words.
She is a sutra-reciting woman from the world of light;
She will answer questions about the Diamond Sutra."
    When the commander of ghosts heard this message,
He allowed lady Wang who reads the sutras to pass.

When they had passed this Pass of Ghost Gate,
They arrived, pressing on, at the field of iron dogs.
There she saw seven iron dogs with bulging eyes,
Resembling tigers and wolves with teeth of steel.
    They blocked the road and wouldn't let lady Wang pass;
They got Fifth Daughter Wang who reads the sutras.
Lady Wang was filled with fear at the sight and,
Seated in lotus position, recited the Diamond Sutra.
    When she had recited all of the Diamond Sutra,
The iron dogs each went off in a different direction.

When they had passed this field with its iron dogs,
They arrived, pressing on, at the river called "Alas!"
Gods of the soil protecting the bridge, seated on both sides,
All asked, "You, woman! Which village are you from?"
    The virgin lads answered the gods of the soil as follows:
"Gods of the soil protecting the bridge, please listen!
Let me tell you, this woman here with us today is
No one else but Fifth Daughter Wang who reads the sutras!"
    Hearing this, these gods of the soil expressed their respect,
And they promptly guided Fifth Daughter across the river.
Those who are without sin cross over the bridge, but
Those who are burdened by sin are thrown into the river.
    Once, scheming and conniving, they arrive here,
They are kicked off the bridge to suffer a terrible fate—
The sinners below the bridge count in the millions, and
All shackled and chained they suffer a truly terrible fate!
    When lady Wang lowered her head to have a good look,
They turned out to be evil sinners from the world of light.
The sinners down in the lake addressed her as follows:
"Dear woman who cultivated goodness, please listen to us!
    You practiced ample goodness while in the world of light,
Whereas we, while in the world of light, were intent on evil,
Claiming that in the underworld none would bear witness—
But retribution, alas, does not make the slightest mistake!"
    The woman lady Wang spoke to them in the following way:

"You sinners down there in the lake, please listen to me.
In the world of light you all did not practice good deeds, but
You beat monks, cursed priests, and did not burn incense.

You wore on your heads a hat seven inches tall
And pretended to be exorcists, became master exorcists.
You ate your fill of the rice you received from people,
But on the first and the fifteenth you didn't burn any lamps.

You didn't rise in the fifth watch to beat the bronze drum,
Nor did you go and burn incense in front of the Buddha.
You did not go and recite sutras in front of the Buddha, but
Each day you slept and snored till the sky was bright.

In the world of light you enjoyed a life of ample blessing,
But in the underworld you are unable to cross the river Alas.
When interrogated by King Yama, you'll know no sutra:
You've been kicked off the bridge to suffer a terrible fate!

But because I cannot bear to see you in this suffering,
I will recite the Diamond Sutra here below the bridge."

When she had recited the Diamond in nineteen scrolls,
She had saved all these sinners to the very last soul.
Each and every sinner was freed of his shackles, and
Each and every sinner thanked Fifth Daughter Wang.

When they had passed the bridge across the river Alas,
They arrived, pressing on, at Precious Mirror Mountain.
There were three roads on Precious Mirror Mountain:
Two of these roads were black, and one of them bright.

When those burdened with sin arrive at this spot,
They're led toward the black roads, to go in darkness.

When they had passed the Precious Mirror Mountain,
They arrived, pressing on, at Toward-Town Mountain.

Arriving there, she was questioned in the Five Halls:
That interrogation by the Three Lords is awe inspiring.
The Lord of Heaven, the Lord of Earth, the Lord of Men:
One's evil crimes and hidden virtues here come to light.

If your fate fits the Lord of Heaven, you go to heaven,

If your fate fits the realm of earth, you see King Yama,
If your fate fits the Lord of Men, man is what you'll be:
Not the slightest mistake can ever be made here!
    This woman lady Wang had done many good deeds
And never committed any evil: set for the blue sky!
But when the Three Lords then looked into her case,
It turned out she had damaged one Diamond Sutra!
    She had cut off nine characters of a Diamond Sutra,
Which shortened her mortal life by twice twenty years.
Lady Wang had been destined to live till seventy-two,
But at thirty-two she was summoned to see King Yama!

When she had passed Toward-Town and been interrogated,
She arrived at the first underworld court and its judge.
    This infernal judge is in charge of the mountain of swords;
The sufferings of that mountain of swords are unbearable!
Those who are burdened by sin are cut up by these swords,
But lady Wang, who practiced virtue, was allowed to pass.

Lady Wang then arrived at the second underworld court;
The infernal judge of this second court was King First River.
    After submitting one's record of sin and virtue while alive,
One may enjoy the vats of boiling oil of the underworld.
Those who are burdened by sin pass through the vats of oil—
Lady Wang, who was free of sin, was spared the vats of oil.

The virgin lads led her to the third underworld court, and
Presented her to the Song Imperial King of the third court.
    The third court is in charge of the fields of freezing ice
And of its wild ox-headed demons and horse-faced fiends.
Those who are burdened by sin are sent to this field of ice:
Their heads are covered with snow; their feet walk on frost.
    Once lady Wang had been witness to their sufferings,
She could not stop herself from crying and said,
"In the world of light you neglected to practice goodness,
Not knowing that later your sufferings would be unbearable."

Lady Wang then arrived in the fourth underworld court;
The ruler of the fourth court is the King of Five Senses.
All those who were scandalmongers in the world of light
Here have their tongues ripped out and tied to their stomachs.

The virgin lads led the way as they walked, pressing on,
And so they reached the fifth court, that of King Yama.
     The fifth underworld court is in charge of four vats of oil;
The torment of bronze drum and iron pillar is unbearable![14]
Those burdened by sin are pushed below the bridge of blood—
Tens and tens of times the bronze drum and the iron pillar!

Lady Wang was a person of goodness, and she easily passed,
And so they arrived at the sixth court, of the King of Full Change,
Who strangles your three souls and your seven spirits—
Those who are good will rise again; the evil ones perish.

Lady Wang then arrived at the seventh underworld court;
The ruler of the seventh court is the King of Mount Tai.
The famous ruler of this court has millstones turned,
And evil men are here reduced to utter nothingness!

Walking on, lady Wang arrived at the eighth underworld court;
The judge of this eighth court was the King of Fair Balance.
     Those who take with a big bushel but pay with a small one
Are here dismembered by lance and sword for their vile sin.
All their accumulated gold and silver here is of no use at all:
Punishments in the underworld bring unbearable pain.

She then arrived at the ninth court, that of the King of the Market.
This infernal court chastises those who are far too rich.
In front of the palace hall a bronze pillar has been erected,
Its top heated red-hot with fire, like the iron beds.
     Those who are burdened by sin are without number, and for
Those who have committed evil on earth, no pardon exists.
It is only those who practiced goodness all through their lives
Who from a bottomless fiery pit will rise straight to heaven.

Pressing on, the woman lady Wang continued her journey
And arrived at the tenth court, that of the Wheel-turning King.
He promptly ordered his associate judges to get out her file—
Promptly found: "Fifth Daughter Wang who read the sutras."

They found that her mortal life was to have been seventy-two years;
She now appeared in front of the judge before her destined time.
The associate judges hastily reported in a memorial, stating:
"Your Majesty, please listen well to what we have to say.

Lady Wang was a sutra-reciting woman of the world of light;
She's been brought here to answer questions on the Diamond.
Because she damaged nine characters of a Diamond Sutra,
Her mortal life was shortened by twice twenty years."

When the infernal judge heard them tell him this story,
He promptly dispatched lady Wang back to the world of light.
The associate judge in charge of the records then stated:
"Your Majesty, please listen to what I have to say.

In the Eastern Capital lives a certain millionaire Zhang;
He is immensely rich as the owner of many fields and farms.
The millionaire's wife is a daughter of the Kong family;
By building bridges and paving roads, she seeks a son.

Husband and wife have made a vow to accumulate merit,
Unhappy because they have no child to manage their wealth."

The infernal judge, hearing this report of the associate judge,
Thereupon told Fifth Daughter Wang who reads the sutras:
"I here today decide to send you back to the world of light,
Changed from a woman into a man, back to the world of light."
When lady Wang heard this, she hastened to make a bow,
With lowered head made four bows before the infernal judge,

And said, "As you are sending me back to the world of light,
There are some issues that I'd like to bring to your attention.
I will not go and be reborn in the regions of foreign countries
Because the languages of those barbarians are hard to decipher.

I will not go and be reborn in a family of the butchers' guild,
Because once I have grown up, I'll slaughter pigs and goats.
I will not go and be reborn in the family of a blacksmith,
Because once I have grown up, I'll make lances and swords.

Sending me now, you'd better let me be a sedan-chair carrier;
In that profession I'd feel most at ease, like an ant on sugar!
Or send me to a pious family that practices good deeds,
Because once I have grown up, I'll just write essays."

When the infernal judge had heard her tell this story,
He said to her, "Dear pious woman, Fifth Daughter Wang,
As you practiced virtue, you'll enjoy riches and longevity;
I will see to it that you are reborn as the son of a millionaire!"

When lady Wang heard these words, she made a deep bow
And also thanked the associate judge in charge of the records.

After she had left the infernal courts of the underworld,
The four virgin lads again escorted Fifth Daughter Wang.
Changing her into a peach from the land of the immortals,
They took her to the Eastern Capital's Zhang Family Village.

In the third watch of the night lady Kong had a dream,
And in her dream her mouth tasted an immortal peach.
In her dream lady Kong swiftly swallowed that peach,
And so, all of a sudden, she found herself to be pregnant.

After she had been pregnant for almost a full year,
She gave birth to a baby boy who was really exceptional.
When they poured water into a golden bowl for his bath,
They found on one of his legs three columns of writing,

Which read, "I hail from Nanhui County in Caozhou,
From Zhao Family Village in the township of Qingping.
The name by which I myself am known is lady Wang;
The husband I was married to was named Zhao Lingfang.

I gave birth to one baby boy and also one baby girl:
The name that was selected for that boy was Xiaoyu;
The name that was selected for the girl was Xinxiang.

I, woman Wang, died at the age of thirty-two years;
Despite my sutra recitation, my life did not last long.
Fortunately, we were originally a loving couple—
Transformed from a woman into a man, I arrive here."

On the third day a name was selected for the little boy;
The name chosen for the baby was Sibao.

From infancy he displayed a remarkable intelligence,
And at the early age of twelve he entered a school.
"Dear teacher, please select a fitting name for me!"
"The name I choose to call you is Zhang Shifang!"

First he read common words: "fish," "hill," and "stream."
And then he read *The Classic of Filial Piety* all the way through.
Upon reading the Classics, he knew the meaning of rites,
And he memorized hundreds and thousands of essays.

When the county instructor held his examination,
He passed as both a civil and a military aspiring student,
And when he had submitted three well-crafted essays,
He was registered as the new student Zhang Shifang.

Shifang went home and told his father and mother,
"Dear father and mother, please listen to my words.
A placard has been posted in the Eastern Capital,
And it summons all students from the whole world.

I will go to the Eastern Capital to take the examination,
Leaving you, my parents, in charge of fields and farms.
If I obtain an office, I will return in three years,
But otherwise I'll be back home within six months."

The parents answered their son in the following way:
"Dear son, now please listen to what we have to say.

If you want to seek an office, hurry up and go quickly,
And come back home once you've obtained a fine post.
We are now advanced in years and find it hard to walk,
So who can manage the family wealth on our behalf?"

As soon as Shifang had heard this, he took his leave—
All of a sudden his cheeks were wet, awash in tears!
In one day he traveled fifty miles from his home, and
In two days he traveled twice fifty miles from his home.

After crossing some fords, there were again some fords;
After passing one mountain, there waited another hill.
In my song I cannot mention each stretch of the journey,
But he arrived at the Eastern Capital with its fine walls.

Once he had entered the Eastern Capital, he found it was
A wonderful place with its miles on end of red mansions!

He also found there [an innkeeper], a man surnamed Li;
"Please take me on a tour and show me all the wards!"
    There was no end to the sights of the Eastern Capital,
But his heart was exclusively set on reading the books.
The placard was posted on the fifteenth of the Seventh Month,
He sat for the examination on the fifteenth of the Eighth Month.
    In the first session some tens of students were chosen;
In the second session double the number was selected.
Because his three fine essays met all requirements,
He became the Henan provincial candidate Zhang Shifang.
    He sat for the capital exams in the Third Month following
And passed with highest honors, which was quite an honor.
The emperor declared him, with his own imperial brush,
Declared him to be Top-of-the-List Zhang Shifang.
    His Majesty personally offered him three cups of wine;
On horseback he paraded through town, to the city god's temple.
All officials at court came and offered their congratulations,
And they also sent him presents, including pigs and goats.

Receiving these, the top of the list was very pleased;
With what glory and status did he return to his home!
    Incense was burned in his honor all along the main street,
While he burned three sets of incense to thank Heaven.
With the first he thanked Heaven, with the second Earth;
With the third he thanked his parents for raising him.
    But even though he had succeeded as top of the list,
He also pondered the three columns of writing on his leg.
"How ridiculous it is to be obsessed with those lines:
The Wang family in Caozhou should be my old home!"
    Eventually Shifang came up with a plan in his heart;
He wanted to write a request addressed to the Throne.
He had no inclination at all to be the top of the list
But wanted very much to make the journey to Caozhou.
    "Your servant was a daughter of the Caozhou Wangs;
The husband I was married to was Zhao Lingfang, but
    At the age of thirty-two I passed away, whereupon I
Visited the ten courts of justice in the underworld.

As I had practiced many good deeds, the judge had me
Be reborn in the Eastern Capital's Zhang Family Village."
    When the emperor read this request, he showed a smile
And promptly appointed Shifang prefect of Caozhou.
He awarded him a purple gown and a golden girdle—
Bronze clubs and bronze axes arranged on both sides!
    Shifang came and expressed his gratitude to his lord,
Wishing him many times a myriad years of long life.
Upon taking his leave from the emperor, he set out,
The only thought in his mind to visit his hometown!

The men who carried his luggage—more than a hundred!
They escorted the top of the list appointed as prefect.
Whenever he passed through a prefecture or a county,
He was warmly welcomed by all the local officials.
    In this way, he made rapid progress all through his trip
Until he arrived in the prefectural office of Caozhou.
The county magistrate of Nanhui warmly welcomed him,
And the two officials met him with smiles on their faces.
    Once the top of the list had assumed his position,
He ordered two runners of the Caozhou prefecture:
    "You two have to leave this prefectural city and go
To the township of Qingping in the county of Nanhui.
Tell the old man Lingfang to appear here in court,
As there is a matter on which he will be interrogated."

The two government runners went on their way,
And, pressing on, they arrived in Zhao Family Village.
"The top of the list is now the prefect of Caozhou
And orders the presence of Zhao Lingfang, butcher."
    When Zhao Lingfang heard them bring this message,
His face turned as yellow as earth because he was scared:
"I must have committed some crime in killing pigs—
What does the top of the list want me to suffer?"
    He hastily called out his son and his daughter.
"My dear children, please listen to what I have to say.
Four government runners have arrived from Caozhou;

I don't know what kind of hardship I'll have to suffer."
When his son and daughter heard him talk like this,
[They said,] "Please do not worry yourself as you go!
Throughout your life you never have cheated anyone;
At midnight you are at ease even with an open gate."
Zhao Lingfang was beset by all kind of anxieties;
He pleaded with the ancestors and the god of the stove
And also called upon lady Wang in the underworld
To protect him in Caozhou when seeing the prefect.
"If we have an affinity, please save me from death—
If we have no affinity, I'll lose my life away from home.
If I am fated to die over there in Caozhou Prefecture,
Please transport my remains back home for burial."
When his children heard this, they were awash in tears,
And they decided to accompany their father on his trip.
They took their leave of their close and distant relatives
And said good-bye to the place called Zhao Family Village.

When they arrived in Caozhou to meet with the prefect,
The government runners entered first to report their arrival.
When the prefect learned Zhao Lingfang had arrived,
He promptly spoke, "You, old man, now listen to me!
Today I have called you here for no other reason but
To interrogate you about one single fact of your life.
To which family did your wife, the lady Wang, belong?
And how many sons and daughters did she bear you?"
Zhao Lingfang answered then in the following words:
"Your Excellency, please listen to my explanation.
The wife I married was a woman of the Wang family
Who passed away at the age of only thirty-two years.
She left behind one pair, a baby boy and a baby girl
Who've come here with me to Your Excellency's court."
When the prefect heard these words from Zhao Lingfang,
He showed him the three columns of writing on his leg;
He displayed the three columns of writing on his leg;
He showed him the three columns of writing on his leg.
"I am none else than your wife, Fifth Daughter Wang!

Transformed from a woman into a man, a top of the list!
But I did not want at all to be the top of the list, so I
Immediately submitted a request to our lord and king."

Now that they indeed had been reunited, the prefect
Promptly asked where lady Wang had been buried.
The prefect wanted to go and see the burial site,
So they went there together, by horse and sedan chair.

"My remains from an earlier life are all buried here;
Now in this life I have become the top of the list!"
Using a crane, they promptly raised the coffin, and
When they opened the coffin they saw one woman.

The coffin and the corpse dissolved right away—
The top of the list shed tears that fell profusely.

The family of four, mother and son, practiced goodness;
He did not return to court to protect his king and lord.
The Jade Emperor issued an edict informing all four
That they would live their lives in the Western Paradise.

In one life she practiced goodness as a woman, and
In the next life she cultivated herself: top of the list!
She lives in a dragon palace at the bottom of the ocean,
And throughout the world her fame is renowned.

NOTES

INTRODUCTION: WOMEN'S SCRIPT

1   For writings by women of traditional China, see Idema and Grant 2004. The eighteenth-century author Shi Zhenlin (1692–1778) provided in the pages of his *Random Records of West Green* (Xi Qing sanji), an intimate and detailed portrait of the peasant poet Shuangqing, quoting many of her lyrics, but modern scholarship outside China tends to see her as a creature of fiction (Choi 1993; Fong 1997; Ropp 2001; Idema and Grant 2004, 520–41).

2   Zhao Liming 1992, 15–16.

3   Gong 1995.

4   Bai and Xiang 2004, 62–89.

5   As song, the texts in women's script show many similarities to women's bridal and funeral laments. For those collected from Hong Kong, see Blake 1978; Johnson 1988, 2003; Watson 1996; and Ho 2005. For those from Nanhui (near Shanghai), see McLaren 2000, 2003. However, because the women themselves wrote down the texts in women's script, the texts are longer and more deliberately composed.

6   Lu Banü, the author of one autobiographical ballad, describes being taken out of school at the instigation of her future husband's family (Zhao Liming 1992, 349).

7   The 1995 local Jiangyong gazetteer mentions "prayers to the gods" in first place, suggesting that many more religious texts existed at one time (Hunan sheng 1995, 610).

8   Translations of texts in some of these categories are provided in Chiang 1995, 219–

77; and Idema and Grant 2004, 543–66. The most comprehensive Western-language anthology is Idema 1996.

9 The local cultural worker Zhou Shuoyi played an important intermediary role, occasionally assisting these women to such an extent that he should be considered a cowriter.

10 Gong 1991, 25.

11 See, for example, Silber 1994; and Chiang 1995.

12 For more on this contextual approach to women's script writings, see Fei-wen Liu 2001, 2004a, 2004b; and Liu Feiwen 2003a, 2003b, 2005.

13 The novel is *Snow Flower and the Secret Fan,* by Lisa See.

14 Yao and Zhong 1929.

15 Liu and Hu 1994; and Ji 2006.

16 Liu and Hu 1994, 311.

17 See, for example, Liang 1995.

18 Liu and Hu 1994, 309.

19 McLaren 1996, 400, 411.

20 Liu Feiwen 2005.

21 Zhao Liming 1992, 758–60. Zhao notes that the text was "edited" by Zhou Shuoyi.

22 Xie Zhimin 1991, 1836; and Liu Feiwen 2005, 97–101.

23 In China, a pregnancy is said to take ten months, counting from the month in which the woman conceives to the month in which the baby is born.

24 Zhao Liming 1992, 718–23. One may note that this text, too, was "edited" by Zhou Shuoyi.

25 Ibid., 723–29.

26 Ibid., 755–58. Again, the text was edited by Zhou Shuoyi.

27 Demiéville 1959.

28 Zhongguo Quyizhi Quanguo Bianji Weiyuanhui 1992, 115.

29 Zhao Liming 1992, 691–718.

30 Ibid., 670–71.

31 Liu Nianci 1986, 152–58; Wang Anqi 1990; and Kuzay 1995, 254–71, 317–57.

32 Zhao Liming 1992, 799–812.

33 O'Hara 1945, 141–43.

34 Diény 1977.

35 For the fragment, see Zhao Liming 1992, 504–6; Zhao does not classify this item as an adaptation of a songbook text, and its heroine is alternately called "lady Guan" and "lady Luo." For the version handwritten by Gao Yinxian, see ibid., 677–91. For the adaptation transcribed by Yi Nianhua, see ibid., 671–76.

36 Ibid., 690.

37 Idema 2008.

38 O'Hara 1945, 113–15.

39 For example, see Wang Ch'iu-kuei 1977, 1978, 1979, 1981; and Idema 2008.

40 For the shorter version, see Zhao Liming 1992, 667–70. For the longer version, see ibid., 655–66.

41 Studies on Judge Bao in vernacular literature are very numerous but focus on his role in drama and fiction (Bauer 1974, 1992; Hayden 1978; Ma 1973, 1975). The authors of many of these studies did not have access to the fifteenth-century ballads that deal with Judge Bao or the late-sixteenth-century one-hundred-chapter novel about the judge (Hanan 1980). For partial translations of a late-nineteenth-century novel about Judge Bao based on adaptations by nineteenth-century storytellers, see Shi 1998; and Shi and Yu 1997.

42 Zhao Liming 1992, 775–99.

43 Ibid., 813–16.

44 McLaren 1996, 402, 411.

45 Zhao Liming 1992, 506–7.

46 McLaren 1996, 409.

47 Their actual behavior was determined by a host of contextual factors (Fei-wen Liu 2001).

48 See, for example, Yang and Yang 1956; Boesken 1984; Zhang Henshui 1991; Altenburger 2005; and Grant 1989.

49 For the fragment of the Liang Shanbo and Zhu Yingtai story in women's script, see Zhao Liming 1992, 760–61.

50 In this respect, Zhu Yingtai is different from the heroines of the *tanci,* or long verse narratives, written by eighteenth- and nineteenth-century elite women. These heroines as a rule are forced to dress as men in order to flee the machinations of a villain. The elite authors of *tanci* indulge in their fantasies as their heroines (still in male disguise) go on to success in the examinations and outperform men both at court and on the battlefield (Idema and Grant 2004, 717–63).

51 Zhao Liming 1992, 762–74.

52 In the *tanci* written by elite women of the eighteenth and nineteenth centuries, the female identity of the heroine in male disguise often is discovered when her bound feet, which earlier had been hidden in boots, are exposed (ibid., 739).

53 See Grant 1989.

54 Zhao Liming 1992, 729–55.

1. ADMONITIONS FOR MY DAUGHTER

1 Chinese characters often consist of one element denoting the general category of the word's meaning (the radical) and another element suggesting the pronunciation.

2   Jing Jiang was the mother of Wen Bo, a contemporary of Confucius in the state of Lu. She imposed strict discipline on her son and considered constant industry a major source of a moral life. When her son suggested that she did not need to spin because of his exalted official position, she berated him at length. She has one of the longest entries in Liu Xiang's *Biographies of Exemplary Women*, in the chapter "Biographies Illustrating the Correct Deportment of Mothers."

2.   THE TEN MONTHS OF PREGNANCY

1   Double-Five is the fifth day of the Fifth Month. The day is celebrated with boat races in memory of attempts to rescue the ancient poet Qu Yuan, who committed suicide by drowning himself in a river.

2   Upon death, the soul of the deceased has to appear before the ten judges of the underworld. These judges may be collectively designated King Yama, but the term may also refer more specifically to the highest of the ten judges.

3   The grandmother here is the mother of the child's mother.

4   Here, the Third Day is the second day following the day on which the baby was born. If that date happens to be an unlucky day according to the almanac, the Third Day may also be celebrated later.

5   Fright was traditionally seen as the cause of many childhood diseases.

6   Traditionally, Chinese babies did not wear diapers but split pants.

3.   THE FAMILY HEIRLOOM

1   In order to mislead jealous ghosts and to improve a child's fortune, parents might have their child formally adopted by other people who for whatever reason are believed to offer the child greater protection. These "dry parents" would be rewarded for this service.

2   Weddings were, and still are, most lavishly celebrated. Outside observers have often remarked that families incur huge debts in order to throw lavish weddings. From a Buddhist perspective, the parents commit a grave sin out of love for their child when they allow the killing of animals whose meat will be served to guests.

3   Jiangyong is one of the many areas in rural southern China that practice delayed-transfer marriage, in which, following the wedding, the bride returns to her parents and visits her parents-in-law only on festival days. Once she has become pregnant, she moves in for good with her parents-in-law and husband.

4   The meaning of this line is unclear to me. We could perhaps associate the snow with death, as white is the color of mourning.

5   The translation of this line is very tentative, and the meaning eludes me.

6 Following death, the soul of the deceased has to appear before each of the ten courts of the underworld: the soul appears before the first judge on the seventh day following his or her death, before the second on the fourteenth, before the third on the twenty-first, before the fourth on the twenty-eighth, before the fifth on the thirty-fifth, before the sixth on the forty-second, and before the seventh on the forty-ninth. The soul of the deceased then appears before the eighth judge on the one hundredth day following his or her death, before the ninth judge one full year after his or her death, and before the final tenth judge three years (actually twenty-seven months) after his or her death. Filial offspring may help the soul of the deceased in passing these hurdles on the road toward rebirth by inviting Buddhist monks to recite sutras, because some of the merit generated by the reciting of sutras may offset some of the sins of the deceased and mitigate the punishment for these sins. Because the interval between the first seven ceremonies is seven days, such funeral rituals are called the "Sevens." Not all families were capable or willing to pay for a full set of Sevens.

7 The text of this line is incomplete, and the translation is therefore tentative.

8 Thunder and lightning were believed to be caused by Thunder, a winged deity wielding a hammer.

9 The person who passed the triennial metropolitan and palace examinations with highest honors was designated top of the list, or *zhuangyuan,* and could look forward to a brilliant career in the administration.

10 Meng Zong was widely known as one of the Twenty-four Exemplars of Filial Piety. When his evil stepmother wanted to eat bamboo shoots in the middle of winter, he went out to search for them, and in answer to his sincere prayers, bamboo shouts sprouted despite the freezing cold.

11 Dong Yong is another of the Twenty-four Exemplars of Filial Piety. Upon the death of his father, he sold himself as a slave so that he could provide his father with a fitting funeral. Moved by his filial piety, the highest god dispatched the Weaving Maid (Vega) from heaven to help him pay back his debt and regain his freedom.

12 Zhao Wuniang is a filial daughter-in-law in *The Story of the Lute* (Pipa ji), a long play by Gao Ming (ca. 1307–ca. 1371). After her husband departs for the capital to take the metropolitan examinations, she serves her parents-in-law most obediently. When they die from starvation during a famine, she buries them with her own hands and sells her beautiful long hair to pay for the expenses. She then travels to the capital, making her way by begging, and is eventually reunited with her husband.

4. THE LAZY WIFE

1 The Western Han dynasty ruled China from 206 B.C.E. to 8 C.E., the Eastern Han dynasty ruled from 23 to 220, and the Tang dynasty ruled from 617 to 906. A list

of subjects listeners will not hear about is a common opening formula in ballad literature.

2   In traditional China, white was the color of mourning, and mourning clothes were made of coarse hemp.

5. THE TALE OF THIRD SISTER

1   The Guangxu period lasted from 1875 to 1908.

2   Those who passed the lowest level of the state examinations, at the prefectural level, were formally admitted to the prefectural school and became "students."

3   The eight characters are the four pairs of two cyclical characters used to identify the year, month, day, and hour of one's birth. The five elements refer to metal, wood, water, fire, and earth, which follow and conquer one another.

4   Zhu Maichen (d. 115 B.C.E.) suffered dire poverty for many years. Eventually his wife requested a divorce and married a butcher. When Zhu Maichen later was called to court and returned to his home region as governor, his wife wanted to go back to him. Zhu Maichen then spilled some water on the ground and told her that she could become his wife again if she could retrieve the spilled water. The story was widely known.

5   Lü Mengzheng (946–1011) was a high official of the Song dynasty. Legend has it that he lived in the greatest poverty as a young student. When the daughter of the prime minister chose a husband by throwing a colored ball into a crowd of suitors, Lü caught the ball. The prime minister refused to accept Lü as a son-in-law, but his daughter followed the young man and lived with him in a dilapidated kiln. Later Lü passed the metropolitan examinations with highest honors.

6   Wang Baochuan was, according to legend, the daughter of a prime minister during the Tang dynasty (617–906). She also remained loyal to her husband, the lowly soldier Xue Pinggui, during the eighteen years when he served on the border. Eventually Xue Pinggui would marry a barbarian princess and become the ruler of the state of Xiliang. He then returned to be reunited with Wang Baochuan.

7   Bound feet were often described as "three-inch golden lotuses."

8   Literally, "Straddling the Lintel of the Door."

9   Great White is the planet Venus, which is associated with the element metal. The astral lord of Great White often descends to earth in disguise and helps deserving people.

10 Some lines of text seem to be missing here. From the context, it would appear that the astral lord of Great White appears to Third Sister and her husband in a dream and tells them where to find a hidden treasure.

1   The Later (or Eastern) Han ruled from 23 to 220.

2   A *kasaya* is a monk's robe.

3   The Book of Changes is one of the Five Classics (here designated the Five Works). The Book of Odes and the Book of Documents also belong to the Five Classics. The Four Books are *The Analects, Mencius, The Great Learning,* and *The Central Mean.*

4   The bodhisattva Guanyin in her female manifestation is often depicted holding a willow wand in one hand and a vase of sweet dew in the other.

5   Zhang Guolao and Lü Dongbin are two of the famous Eight Immortals.

6   The wishes accompanying the second and third cups of wine have apparently dropped out of the text.

7   Both Zhao Liming and Xie Zhimin transcribe the last three characters of this line as *wang wang ji,* which can only be translated as "Wang Wangji," but such a person is not known from other versions of the tale (Zhao Liming 1992, 805; Xie Zhimin 1991, 1523). I suggest that these three characters might be a mistake and should have been *yuan huangdi* (Emperor Yuan).

8   On New Year's Day the whole family should be united, as the younger generations wish the older generations a happy new year.

9   "A horse growing horns" is a common simile for something impossible. When Prince Dan of Yan was kept captive in Qin and asked permission to return to his native country, the king of Qin, later the First Emperor, told him that he would allow him to go home only if crows had white heads and horses grew horns. When Prince Dan prayed to Heaven, the heads of crows turned white and horses grew horns, and the king of Qin was forced to set him free. I am unaware of any story linking a king of Qi with horses growing horns.

10 Great White is the planet Venus, associated with the element metal, which shines brilliantly as the Evening Star or the Morning Star. In popular literature, the astral lord of Great White often descends to earth in the guise of a friendly old man to help deserving characters.

11 The translation of this line is tentative. I take it to mean "in order not to set out on his trip when pine and cypress would already have been planted at his parents' graves."

12 The text actually reads "The official promptly answered the woman as follows," but that is an obvious mistake here.

13 The text of these two lines is clearly mixed up.

14 The translation of this line is a guess. For "third on the list" *(tanhua lang),* the text reads "reunion meeting" *(tuanyuan hui),* which does not make sense to me here.

1   According to one Chinese legend on the origin of the universe, the world was made from the body parts of the giant Pangu following his death.

2   The golden steps leading up to the throne.

3   Tripitaka of the Tang is the Buddhist monk Xuanzang (602–684), who, from 629 to 645, traveled though Central Asia and modern India searching for Buddhist scriptures. Upon his return to China, he devoted the remaining years of his life to translation work. Later legend turned this pilgrimage to the holy places of Buddhism into a pilgrimage to the Western Heavenly Paradise of the Buddha. The story was repeatedly adapted for the stage and in the sixteenth century became a one-hundred-chapter novel, *The Journey to the West* (Xiyou ji), usually ascribed to one Wu Cheng'en.

4   Mulian (Maudgalyayana) was one of the first generation of disciples of the Buddha and was especially renowned for his supernatural powers. In China, legend has it that he became a monk after the death of his parents. He then discovered that his father was living in heaven but his mother had been condemned to suffer the most terrible tortures of hell for the sins she had committed during her lifetime. With the help of the Buddha, Mulian eventually succeeded in liberating his mother from hell. This legend was linked to the Buddhist Ghost Festival on the fifteenth day of the Seventh Month. The tale of Mulian was already part of Buddhist storytelling in the eighth century and would continue to be told until modern times; from the eleventh century onward, it was also adapted for the stage and developed into China's most popular and most spectacular mystery play.

5   It is not clear which story is intended here—this is perhaps a reference to the tale of the filial son Dong Yong.

6   Ding Lan is said to have lived during the Han. He is one of the Twenty-four Exemplars of Filial Piety. Filled with longing for his mother after her death, he carved a wooden image in her likeness.

7   Lady Xiao remained loyal to her husband despite an absence of eighteen years. Her story is told in chapter 7 of this volume.

8   Zhu Yingtai dressed as a man so that she could study at an academy and fell in love with her roommate Liang Shanbo. When her parents promised her to someone else, Liang Shanbo fell ill and died, and Zhu Yingtai jumped into his grave. Her story is told in chapter 11 of this volume.

9   Meng Jiangnü's husband was arrested and deported to the north, where he worked as a conscript laborer on the Great Wall; he soon died and was buried in the body of the wall. When winter approached, Meng Jiangnü set out to bring her husband some winter clothes. When she found out her husband had died, she brought down the Great Wall with her weeping. Her story is told in chapter 8 in this volume.

10   The bodhisattva Guanyin was venerated in female form in China from the eleventh
     century onward. She was considered the embodiment of seductive female beauty.

8.   THE MAIDEN MENG JIANG

According to Zhao Liming, "This song is a common popular narrative ballad
(changben). In 1986 it was transcribed into women's script by Yi Nianhua and Zhou
Shuoyi" (Zhao Liming 1992, 666).

1   First Night is the first full moon of the year, the fifteenth of the First Month. The
     Lantern Festival is celebrated on this night.

2   Guansheyin is Guanyin, the bodhisattva of mercy, who is often depicted as a beau-
     tiful young woman. The little island of Putuoshan off the Zhejiang coast was a major
     center of her cult.

3   In ballad literature, "Eastern Capital" (Dongjing) is the common designation for
     Kaifeng as the capital of the Northern Song dynasty (960–1126). Here it seems to
     be used in the general sense of capital.

4   The modern editor of the text observes that this contradicts the earlier information
     that Fan Qilang hailed from Nanyang in Dengzhou.

5   Chang'an was the capital of both the Western Han dynasty (206 B.C.E–8 C.E.) and
     the Tang dynasty (617–906). Here it is used as a general designation for the na-
     tional capital.

6   Student Zhang and Cui Yingying are the main characters in *Story of the Western
     Wing* (Xixiang ji), China's most popular love comedy. While they are both staying
     temporarily at an out-of-the-way Buddhist monastery, Student Zhang and Ying-
     ying fall in love with each other at first sight. Eventually they have a premarital
     affair, which is discovered by her mother. Student Zhang leaves for the capital to
     take part in the examinations, which he passes with flying colors, and then returns
     to claim Yingying as his bride. The earliest dramatic adaptation of this story is cred-
     ited to Wang Shifu (fl. 1300).

7   Buffalo Herder (Altair) and Weaving Girl (Vega) are two stars on different sides of
     the Heavenly River (Milky Way). According to a widespread legend, the two stars
     are lovers who are allowed to meet only once a year, on the seventh night of the
     Seventh Month, when magpies form a bridge for them across the Heavenly River.

8   The wildflower is a common metaphor for a prostitute.

9   Zhao Wuniang and Cai Yong (Bojie) are the central characters in *The Story of the
     Lute*, by Gao Ming (ca. 1307–ca. 1371). The young student Cai Yong is ordered by
     his father to travel to the capital to take part in the examinations and leaves behind
     his young wife Zhao Wuniang to look after his parents. Cai Yong passes the exam-
     inations with flying colors, but the prime minister then pressures him to marry his

daughter and does not allow him to return home. Meanwhile, a patiently suffering Zhao Wuniang takes care of her suspicious parents-in-law. It is only after they die during a famine that she manages to travel to the capital (begging her way by singing the sad story of her life to the accompaniment of a lute), where she is reunited with her husband and meets his second wife.

10 Middle Prime is also known as the Ghost Festival, as ghosts are welcomed back to their original homes and treated to rich offerings.

11 Li Sanniang and Liu Zhiyuan are the central characters in *The White Hare* (Baitu ji), a very popular play dating from perhaps as early as the fourteenth century. Liu Zhiyuan is a poor farmhand whose future greatness is espied by Li Sanniang and her father. But soon after their marriage, her father dies, and her brothers make life so difficult for Liu Zhiyuan that he decides to join the army, leaving his pregnant wife behind. When a son is born, Li Sanniang has the baby taken to the father, who in the meantime has married the daughter of his commanding officer. When Li Sanniang refuses to remarry, her brothers force her to do the most demanding and demeaning household work. The couple is reunited twelve years later, when Liu Zhiyuan has risen to the rank of provincial governor, and a white hare leads his son to Li Sanniang, his birth mother.

12 This line is incomplete in the original text, and another line of text appears to be missing here.

13 "Kongming" refers to Zhuge Liang, a major character in *Romance of the Three Kingdoms* (Sanguozhi yanyi), an epic prose narrative first printed in the early sixteenth century, which provides an account of the wars in China between 180 and 280. Zhuge Liang is portrayed as not only a wise minister but also a powerful magician.

9. THE FLOWER SELLER

1 During the early decades of the Ming dynasty (1368–1644), local families were charged with the duty of delivering local taxes to the capital or the borders. Many families were ruined by this obligation.

2 The Hanlin Academy was one of the most prestigious organs of the central government, as many of its members served the emperor directly. Only the most promising young officials were appointed to the Hanlin Academy, and such an appointment was generally considered the start of a brilliant career.

3 "Eastern Capital" is the common designation of Kaifeng as the capital of the Northern Song dynasty (960–1126).

4 A baby is said to be one year old from the moment of birth and one year is added to his or her age with each new year. Therefore in Western terms, this baby might be barely one year old.

5   Pressing boards and bamboo splints are instruments of torture.

6   The Yellow Springs are the domain of the dead below the earth.

7   The Nine Springs is one of the many names for the realm of the dead.

8   In contrast to the imperial palace and the organs of the central government, which were located in the northern section of the city, the Kaifeng prefectural offices were located in the southern section of the city.

9   Judge Bao's incognito investigation into the official corruption plaguing famine relief distribution in Chenzhou is one of his better-known adventures. We will learn later that two of the imperial relatives who were sentenced to death by Judge Bao for their part in the corruption scandal were brothers of Empress Cao.

10 Xiao He is credited with establishing the legal code of the Han dynasty (206 B.C.E.– 8 C.E.).

11 The Jade Emperor is the highest deity in the traditional Chinese pantheon.

10. THE DEMONIC CARP

1   After the world was created, it was governed in succession by the Three Emperors (Sanhuang) and the Five Thearchs (Wudi).

2   "Taizu" and "Taizong" were often the posthumous designations for the first two emperors of a dynasty. As this story is set in the Song dynasty, these are probably the founding emperor of the Song dynasty and his successor.

3   The fifteenth of the Eighth Month is celebrated as the Mid-Autumn festival. The season of autumn is associated with the element metal.

4   The word translated here as "squatted down" *(ji)* is defined in the dictionaries as "kneeling down, with upright torso."

5   Demons acquire power over a person after they ingest that person's bodily fluids or fluids that have been in contact with that person. In the much more complicated story of a demonic carp in *The Cases of Judge Bao* (Longtu gong'an), a seventeenth-century collection of the judge's cases, the carp drinks the leftover wine that spills into its pond out of the cup from which the girl has been drinking.

11. THE KARMIC AFFINITY OF LIANG SHANBO AND ZHU YINGTAI

1   Many works of traditional prosimetrical literature start out with a quick summary of Chinese history up to the time in which the story to be told is supposed to have taken place. The summary is here reduced to a single sentence. The Later Han dynasty ruled from 23 to 221.

2   The bodhisattva Guanyin was originally depicted as a handsome young prince but from the Song dynasty (960–1278) onward was increasingly venerated as a beau-

tiful young woman. According to legend, the bodhisattva had lived her mortal life as the princess Miaoshan.

3   Wu Zetian was the wife of the Tang-dynasty emperor Gaozong. Following his death, she eventually reigned in her own name as emperor from 690 to 705.

4   Many versions of this tale here include an episode in which Zhu Yingtai proves to her father that she can pass herself off as a man. She dresses herself as a physician or a fortune-teller, and when her father is taken in by her disguise, he allows her to travel.

5   This contradicts the earlier passage, which states that she had no brothers. In many versions of the tale, Zhu Yingtai has an elder brother whose wife strongly opposes her desire to travel, fearing, she says, that Yingtai will lose her virginity.

6   In some other versions of the tale, too, Liang and Zhu are said to have studied with Confucius (Master Kong).

7   The Dipper is Ursa Major. Like all the other stars and planets, the Dipper is revered as a deity.

8   The word for "to steal" (tou) also has the meaning of conducting an extramarital or premarital affair.

9   The Dragon Gate is the name of rapids in the Yellow River. Carps that were able to cross these rapids against the current were said to turn into dragons. This became a common image for students passing the examinations at the highest level. Here, however, the term may have been used in a quite different meaning: the vagina is often described as a gate, and "one-eyed dragon" is a common designation for the penis. The character *ding* has the shape of a T, and the character for mouth (*kou*) has the shape of a square; together they form the character *ke*, which has the meaning "proper, suitable, admissible." The side of the character *ke* is formed by the character *ding*, that because of its T-shape is also used to designate the male genitalia. One of the few Chinese scholars who has commented on a comparable passage (in which the second line is an answer to Liang's question how deep the river may be) chides it for its obscenity.

10   "Yellow Springs" refers to the underworld.

11   High deities are followed by a golden lad and a jade maiden who act as their servants.

12   King Yama is the most important judge in the underworld.

13   One line of verse appears to be missing here.

12. FIFTH DAUGHTER WANG

1   The Western Han ruled from 206 B.C.E. to 8 C.E., the Eastern Han ruled from 23 to 220, and the Tang dynasty ruled from 617 to 906.

2   Here "Three Pearls" probably refers to the Three Jewels (Buddha, Sangha, and

Dharma), that is, Buddhism. The Twenty-four Exemplars of Filial Piety were celebrated since as early as the Tang dynasty; during the later dynasties they were the subject of one of the most popular children's books.

3   I do not know which specific story is referenced here, but there is no lack of stories about butchers who see the light and abandon their profession. In one version of the legend of Mulian, the holy monk is condemned to be reborn as a butcher because he has allowed the ghosts of many sinners to escape from hell in his first attempt to free his mother from her tortures. Since many of these sinners are reborn as animals, it will be his duty to return them to hell by slaughtering them. During his life as a butcher, Mulian, now called He Yin, is the neighbor of an ostensibly very pious man who succeeds in convincing him to abandon his business. The man turns out to have been a hypocrite all along and ends up being devoured by a tiger, while He Yin follows the bodhisattva Guanyin to the Western Paradise. In expressions like "Zhang San" and "Li Si," the very common surnames Zhang and Li are often used to refer to any Tom, Dick, or Harry.

4   In order to obtain the silk thread, the cocoon is immersed in boiling water, so thousands of living beings are killed in the process of producing enough silk for shoes.

5   Virgin lads are minor deities.

6   That is, the third day after giving birth.

7   The wooden fish is a hollowed-out block of wood carved in the shape of a fish that is used to beat out the rhythm while chanting Buddhist sutras.

8   I have been unable to identify the tale of Shuyu.

9   Because of the merit accruing from Fifth Sister's sincere recitation of the Diamond Sutra, all sinners are freed from their evil karma, and the judges of the underworld have nothing left to do.

10   The god of the stove is usually said to ascend to heaven at the end of the year, when his mouth is smeared with sugar so that he will sweeten his report on the activities of the members of his household.

11   Literally, "like pine and cypress."

12   This line is incomplete, and the translation is tentative.

13   The text has here *podao* (broken knife), obviously a mistake, instead of *poqian* (wasted money).

14   The bronze drum and iron pillar are heated red-hot from the inside before the sinner is tied to them.

CHINESE CHARACTER GLOSSARY

Baitu ji 白兔記
Bao Longtu duan Cao guojiu zhuan 包龍圖斷曹國舅傳
baojuan 寶卷

Cai Yong (Bojie) 蔡邕伯喈
Cao (imperial father-in-law, empress) 曹
Chang'an 長安
changben 唱本
Chuanjiabao 傳家寶
Cui Tingying 崔鶯鶯

Dan (Prince) 丹
ding 丁
Ding Lan 丁蘭
Dong Yong 董永
Dongjing 東京

Fan Qilang 范杞郎
Fan Qiliang 范杞良
Fumu enzhong jing jiangjingwen 父母恩重經講經文

Gao Ming 高明

Gao Yinxian 高銀仙
Guan (Lady) 關
Guansheyin 觀世音
Guanyin 觀音

Han shu 漢書
Hanlin 翰林
He Yin 賀因
Hu Cizhu 胡慈珠
Huang 黃

ji 跽
Jiangyong 江永
Jin ping mei 金瓶梅
Jing Jiang 敬姜

ke 可
Kongming 孔明
kou 口

Lan poniang 懶婆娘
Li Ang 李昂
Li Sanniang 李三娘
Li Si 李四
Liang Shanbo 梁山伯
Liang Zhu yinyuan 梁祝姻緣
Lienü zhuan 列女傳
Liu Sijun 劉思俊
Liu Wenliang 劉文良
Liu Wenlong 劉文龍
Liu Xiang 劉向
Liu Zhiyuan 劉智遠
Liyujing 鯉魚精
Longtu gong'an 龍圖公案
Lu Banü 盧八女
Lu Qiuhu 蘆秋胡
Luoshi nü 羅氏女
Lü Dongbin 呂洞賓
Lü Mengzheng 呂蒙正

Ma 馬
Maihuanü 賣花女
Meng Jiangnü 孟姜女
Meng Zong 孟宗
Miaoshan 妙善
Mulian 目連

nanshu 男書
nüshu 女書

Pangu 盤古
Pipa ji 琵琶記
podao 破刀
poqian 破錢
Pu Bixian 蒲碧仙

Qi Liang 杞良
Qin Luofu 秦羅婦
Qiu Hu 秋胡
Qu Yuan 屈原

Sangu ji 三姑記
sanhuang 三皇
Shafu 殺夫
Shi Zhenlin 史震林
Shiyue huaitai 十月懷胎
Shuangqing 雙卿

Taibai 太白
Taizong 太宗
Taizu 太祖
tanci 彈詞
tanhua lang 探花郎
tou 偷
tuanyuan hui 團圓會

Wang Baochuan 王寶釧
Wang Shifu 王實甫
wang wang ji 王望及

Wang Wuniang 王五娘
Wang Zhaojun 王昭君
Wen Bo 文伯
Wu Cheng'en 吳成恩
Wu Zetian 武則天
wudi 五帝

Xi Qing sanji 西青散記
Xiao He 蕭何
Xiaoshi nü 蕭氏女
Xixiang ji 西廂記
Xiyou ji 西遊記
Xuanzang 玄臧
Xue Pinggui 薛平貴
Xunnü ci 訓女詞

Yang Huanyi 陽煥宜
Yi Nianhua 義年華
yuan huangdi 元皇帝

Zhang (lady, student, butcher) 張
Zhang Guolao 張果老
Zhang San 張三
Zhao Lingfang 趙領方
Zhao Wuniang 趙五娘
Zhou Shuoyi 周碩沂
Zhu Maichen 朱買臣
Zhu Yingtai 祝英台
zhuangyuan 狀元
Zhuge Liang 諸葛良

BIBLIOGRAPHY

Altenburger, Roland. "Is It Clothes That Make the Man? Cross-Dressing, Gender and Sex in Pre-Twentieth-Century Zhu Yingtai Lore." *Asian Folklore Studies* 64 (2005): 165–205.

Bai Gengsheng 白庚胜 and Xiang Yunju 向云驹, eds. *Guizhong qiji: Zhongguo nüshu* 闺中奇迹中国女书 [A miracle of the inner quarters: China's women's script]. Harbin: Heilongjiang renmin chubanshe, 2004.

Bauer, Wolfgang. "'The Tradition of the Criminal Cases of Master Pao,' *Pao-kung-an (Lung-t'u kung-an)*." *Oriens* 23–24 (1974): 433–49.

———, trans. *Die Leiche im Strom: Die seltsame kriminalfälle des Meisters Bao* [The corpse in the river: The rare criminal cases of Judge Bao]. Freiburg, Germany: Herder, 1992.

Blake, Fred. "Death and Abuse in Marriage Laments: The Curse of Chinese Brides." *Asian Folklore Studies* 37 (1978): 13–33.

Boesken, Gerd. *Liang Shanbo und Zhu Yingtai, China's berühmtestes Liebesdrama auf der Bühne der taiwanesische Lokaloper Gezaixi* [Liang Shanbo and Zhu Yingtai: China's most famous love play on the stage of Taiwan local opera Gezaixi]. Taipei: Lucky Books, 1984.

Chiang, William W. *"We Two Know the Script, We Have Become Good Friends": Linguistic and Social Aspects of the Women's Script Literature in Southern Hunan, China.* Lanham, Md.: University Press of America, 1995.

Choi, Elsie. *Leaves of Prayer: The Life and Poetry of He Shuangqing, a Farmwife in Eighteenth-Century China.* Hong Kong: Chinese University Press, 1993.

Demiéville, Paul. "La nouvelle mariée acaciâtre" [The irritable bride]. *Asia Major*, n.s., 7 (1959): 59–65.

Diény, Jean-Pierre. *Pastourelles et magnanarelles: Essai sur un thème littéraire chinois* [Pastoral songs and mulberry-picking songs: A study of a Chinese literary motif]. Geneva: Droz, 1977.

Fong, Grace. "De/Constructing a Feminine Ideal in the Eighteenth Century: *Random Records of West Green* and the Story of Shuangqing." In Ellen Widmer and Kang-I Sun Chang, eds., *Writing Women in Late Imperial China*, 264–81. Stanford, Calif.: Stanford University Press, 1997.

Gong Zhebing 宫哲兵, ed. *Nüshu* 女書 [Women's script]. Taipei: Funü xinzhi jijinhui, 1991.

———. "Nüshu shidai kao" 女书时代考 [On the period of women's script]. In Shi Jinbo 史金波 et al., eds., *Qite di nüshu, Quanguo nüshu xueshu kaocha yanjiuhui wenji* 奇特的女书全国女书学术考察研讨会文集 [The weird women's script: Papers of a national academic conference of research and discussion of women's script], 157–66. Beijing: Beijing Yuyan xueyuan chubanshe, 1995.

Grant, Beata. "The Spiritual Saga of Woman Huang: From Pollution to Purification." In David Johnson, ed., *Ritual Opera, Operatic Ritual, "Mulian Rescues His Mother" in Chinese Popular Culture*, 224–311. Berkeley, Calif.: Chinese Popular Culture Project, 1989.

Hanan, Patrick. "Judge Bao's Hundred Cases Reconstructed." *Harvard Journal of Asiatic Studies* 40, no. 2 (1980): 301–23.

Hayden, George A. *Crime and Punishment in Medieval Chinese Drama: Three Judge Pao Plays*. Cambridge, Mass.: Council on East Asian Studies, Harvard University, 1978.

Ho, Yuk-ying. "Bridal Laments in Rural Hong Kong." *Asian Folklore Studies* 64 (2005): 53–87.

Hunan sheng Jiangyong Xianzhi Biansuan Weiyuanhui 湖南省江永县志编纂委员会. *Jiangyong xianzhi* 江永县志 [Jiangyong county gazetteer]. Beijing: Fangzhi chubanshe, 1995.

Idema, Wilt. *Vrouwenschrift: Vriendschap, huwelijk en wanhoop van Chinese vrouwen, opgetekend in een eigen schrift* [Women's script: Friendship, love, and frustration of Chinese women, recorded in a script of their own]. Amsterdam: Meulenhoff, 1996.

———. "*Changben* Texts in the *Nüshu* Repertoire of Southern Hunan." In Vibeke Børdahl, ed., *The Eternal Storyteller: Oral Literature in Modern China*, 95–114. Richmond, England: Curzon, 1999.

Idema, Wilt L. *Meng Jiangnü Brings Down the Great Wall: Ten Versions of a Chinese Legend*. Seattle: University of Washington Press, 2008.

Idema, Wilt, and Beata Grant. *The Red Brush: Writing Women of Imperial China*. Cambridge, Mass.: Harvard University Asia Center, 2004.

Ji Jun 纪军. "Nüshu xushishi de xushitedian chutan" 女书叙事诗的叙事特点初探 [A preliminary inquiry into the narrative characteristics of narrative poems in women's script]. *Zhongnan minzu daxue xuebao* 中南民族大学学报 26, no. 1 (2006): 167–70.

Johnson, Elizabeth L. "Grieving for the Dead, Grieving for the Living: Funeral Laments of Hakka Women." In James L. Watson and Evelyn S. Rawski, eds., *Death Ritual in Late Imperial and Modern China*, 135–63. Berkeley: University of California Press, 1988.

———. "Singing of Separation, Lamenting Loss: Hakka Women's Expression of Separation and Reunion." In Charles Stafford, ed., *Living with Separation in China: Anthropological Accounts*, 27–52. London: Routledge Curzon, 2003.

Kuzay, Stephan. *Das Nuo von Guichi, Eine Untersuchung zu religiösen Maskenspielen in südlichen Anhui* [The Nuo theater of Guichi, a study of the religious mask plays of southern Anjui]. Frankfurt: Peter Lang, 1995.

Li Ang. *The Butcher's Wife*. Translated by Howard Goldblatt and Ellen Yeung. San Francisco: North Point Press, 1986.

Liang Yao 梁耀. "Nüshu zhong di nüquan yishi" 女书中的女权意识 [Feminist consciousness in the women's script]. In Shi Jinbo et al., eds., *Qite di nüshu*, 195–203. Beijing: Beijing Yuyan xueyuan chubanshe, 1995.

Liu, Fei-wen. "The Confrontation between Fidelity and Fertility: *Nüshu, Nüge*, and Peasant Women's Conceptions of Widowhood in Jiangyong County, Hunan Province, China." *Journal of Asian Studies* 60, no. 4 (2001): 1051–84.

———. "Literacy, Gender, and Class: Nüshu and Sisterhood Communities in Southern Hunan." *Nan Nü* 6, no. 2 (2004a): 241–82.

———. "From Being to Becoming: *Nüshu* and Sentiments in a Chinese Rural Community." *American Ethnologist* 31, no. 3 (2004b): 422–39.

Liu Feiwen 劉斐玟. "Shuxie yu geyong de jiaoshi: Nüshu, nüge yu Hunan Jiangyong funü de shuangchong shewei" 書寫與歌詠的交織女書女歌與湖南江永婦女的雙重視維 [The interweaving of writing and singing: Women's script and women's songs and women's dual vision in Jiangyong county, Hunan Province]. *Taiwan renleixue kan* 臺灣人類學刊 1, no. 1 (2003a): 1–49.

———. "Cong 'yi qing wei yi' dao 'yi you jing zhuan': Hunan Jiangyong nüshu yu 'su kelian'" 從以情為意到意由境轉湖南江永女書與訴可憐 [From "sentiments as statements" to "the meaning of sentiments as context-prompted": Women's script and misery lamentation in Jiangyong county, Hunan Privince]. In *Qing, yu yu wenhua* 情欲與文化 [Love, desire, and culture], edited by Yu Anbang 余安邦, 225–87. Taipei: Zhongyang yanjiuyuan Minzuxue yanjiusuo, 2003b.

———. "Wenben yu wenjingde duihua: Nüshu sanzhaoshu yu funü de qingyi yinsheng" 文本與文境的對話女書三朝書與婦女的情意音聲 [Text, context, and women's voices in women's script Wedding Literature (*Sanzhaozhu*)]. *Taiwan renlei xuekan* 3, no. 1 (2005): 87–142.

Liu Nianci 刘念兹. *Nanxi xinzheng* 南戲新証 [New documents on southern drama]. Beijing: Zhonghua shuju, 1986.

Liu Shouhua and Hu Xiaoshen. "Folk Narrative Literature in Chinese Nüshu: An Amazing New Discovery." *Asian Folklore Studies* 53 (1994): 307–18.

Luo Yihua 罗义华. "Shilun nüshu changci Zhu Yingtai yu Zhuangju Liang Zhu de wenhua chayi" 试论女书唱词祝英台与壮剧梁祝的文化差异 [Cultural differences between the ballad in women's script on Zhu Yingtai and the Zhuang play *Liang and Zhu*]. *Jiang Han daxue xuebao* 江汉大学学报 21, no. 5 (2002): 45–48.

Ma, Y. W. "Themes and Characterization in the *Lung-t'u kung-an*." *T'oung-Pao* 59 (1973): 179–202.

———. "The Textual Tradition of Ming *Kung-an* Fiction: A Study of the *Lung-t'u kung-an*." *Harvard Journal of Asiatic Studies* 35 (1975): 190–220.

McLaren, Anne. "Women's Voices and Textuality. Chastity and Abduction in Chinese Nüshu Writing." *Modern China* 22, no. 4 (1996): 382–416.

———. "The Oral and Ritual Culture of Chinese Women: Bridal Lamentations of Nanhui." *Asian Folklore Studies* 59 (2000): 205–38.

McLaren, Anne E. "Mothers, Daughters, and the Socialization of the Chinese Bride." *Asian Studies Review* 27 (2003): 1–21.

O'Hara, Albert Richard. *The Position of Women in Early China: According to the Lieh Nü Chuan "The Biographies of Eminent Chinese Women."* Washington, D.C.: Catholic University of America Press, 1945. Reprint, Westport, Conn.: Hyperion Press, 1981.

Ropp, Paul S. *Banished Immortal: Searching for Shuangqing, China's Peasant Woman Poet.* Ann Arbor: University of Michigan Press, 2001.

See, Lisa. *Snow Flower and the Secret Fan.* New York: Random House, 2005.

Shi Yukun. *Tales of Magistrate Bao and His Valiant Lieutenants: Selections from "Sanxia wuyi."* Translated by Susan Blader. Hong Kong: Chinese University Press, 1998.

Shi Yukun and Yu Yue. *The Seven Heroes and Five Gallants.* Translated by Song Shou-quan. Beijing: Panda Books, 1997.

Silber, Cathy. "From Daughter to Daughter-in-Law in the Women's Script of Southern Hunan." In Christina Gilmartin et al., eds., *Engendering China: Women, Culture and the State*, 47–68. Cambridge, Mass.: Harvard University Press, 1994.

Wang Anqi 王安祈. "Liu Wenlong xiqu di liuchuan yu yanbian: Ming Xuande xieben *Jinchai ji* suo yinfa di yige wenti" 劉文龍戲曲的流傳與演變明宣德寫本金釵記所-引發的一個問題 [The circulation and development of the plays on Liu Wenlong: A problem raised by the manuscript copy of the Xuande period of the Ming of

The Golden Hairpin]. In *Mingdai xiqu wulun* 明代戲曲五論 [Five studies on Ming drama], 81–99. Taipei: Tai'an chubanshe, 1990.

Wang Ch'iu-kuei. "The Tunhuang Versions of the Meng Chiang-nü Story." *Asian Culture Quarterly* 5, no. 4 (1977): 67–81.

———. "The Formation of the Early Versions of the Meng Chiang-nü Story." *Tamkang Review* 9 (1978): 111–40.

———. "The *Hsiao-shih Meng Chiang Chung-lieh Chen-chieh Hsien-liang Pao-chüan*— An Analytical Study." *Asian Culture Quarterly* 7, no. 4 (1979): 46–72.

———. "From Pao-chüan to Ballad, a Study in Literary Adaptation as Exemplified by Two Versions of the Meng Chiang-nü Story." *Asian Culture Quarterly* 9, no. 1 (1981): 48–65.

Watson, Rubie S. "Chinese Bridal Laments: The Claims of a Dutiful Daughter." In Bell Yung et al., eds., *Harmony and Counterpoint: Ritual Music in Chinese Context*, 107–29. Stanford, Calif.: Stanford University Press, 1996.

Xie Zhimin 谢志民. *Jiangyong nüshu zhi mi* 江永女书之谜 [The mystery of Jiangyong's women's script]. Zhengzhou: Henan Renmin chubanshe, 1991.

Yang Hsien-yi and Gladys Yang, trans. *Love under the Willows, Liang Shan-po and Chu Ying-tai (A Szechuan Opera)*. Beijing: Foreign Languages Press, 1956.

Yao Yizhi 姚逸之 and Zhong Gongxun 鍾貢勛. *Hunan changben tiyao* 湖南唱本提要 [Summaries of songbooks from Hunan], 1929. Reprinted in *Zhongshan daxue minsu congshu* 中山大學民俗叢書 [Sun Yatsen University folklore studies], vol. 9. Taipei: Zhongguo minsu xuehui, 1969.

Zhang Henshui. *The Eternal Love: The Story of Liang Shanbo and Zhu Yingtai*. Translated by S. R. Munro. Singapore: Federal Publications, 1991.

Zhao Li Ming. "The Women's Script of Jiangyong: An Invention of Chinese Women." In Tao Jie et al., eds., *Holding Up Half the Sky: Chinese Women Past, Present, and Future*, 39–52. New York: The Feminist Press at the City University of New York, 2004.

Zhao Liming 赵丽明. *Zhongguo nüshu jicheng* 中国女书集成 [Great collection of China's women's script texts]. Beijing: Qinghua daxue chubanshe, 1992.

———. *Zhongguo nüshu heji* 中國女書合集 [A complete collection of China's women's script texts]. 5 volumes. Beijing: Zhonghua shuju, 2005.

Zhongguo Quyizhi Quanguo Bianji Weiyuanhui 中国曲艺志编辑委员会. *Zhongguo quyi zhi: Hunan juan* 中国曲艺志湖南卷. Beijing: Xinhua chubanshe, 1992.